The Unexpected First

The Unexpected Series

L. Clara

Contents

A Note from the Author

If you or anyone you know is the victim of sexual assault please reach out to RAINN, the National Sexual Assault Telephone Hotline at 800-656-HOPE (4673)

You can also visit **online.rainn.org** to receive support via confidential online chat.

If you are anyone you know is in struggle with substance abuse/addiction, please call the The Recovery Center of america at 888-978-0903

If you or anyone you know is a victim of domestic violence, please reach out for help.

National Domestic Violence Hotline 1-800-799-7233 Text "START" to 88788

If you or anyone you know is struggling with suicidal thoughts or going through a crisis, you can call or text the 988 Lifeline, which provides 24/7, free, and confidential support. Call or text them by dialing 988 or live message/chat with them at their website: https://988lifeline.org

To the person on Facebook who asked for a rec with a spicy scene while on the tattooing table.... you're welcome

Trigger and Content Warnings

Include but are not limited to:

Sexually explicit content

Stalking

Detailed oral rape/sexual assault with a weapon

Hand Necklaces

Tattooing

Sex at a tattoo shop

Murder

Murder in self-defense

Death of a parent

Mention of drugs (no on page use)

Mention of previous suicide attempt and scar covering (not MC)

Mention of previous DV (not MC)

If any of the above warnings may be triggering to you, please do not continue. Your mental health matters more than this story.

Please feel free to reach out to L. Clara at <u>lcturnspages@gmail</u>

.com with any questions regarding triggers.

Playlist

Dancing In The Sky ~ Dani and Lizzy

If this is the last time ~ LANY

Never Say Goodbye ~ Bon Jovi

War Of Hearts~Ruelole

Whole Heart ~ Jessie Reid

Waiting Game ~ BANKS

You Ar The Reasn ~ Calum Scott

Photograph~Ed Sheeran

Evermore ~ Taylor Swift ft Bon Iver

All I Want ~ Kodaline

Figure You Out ~ VOILA

I Like Me Better ~ Lauv

I miss you, I'm sorry ~ Gracie Abrams

Another Love ~ Tom Odelle

Castles ~ Frey Ridings

Back off Bitch ~ Guns N' Roses

I Knew You Were Trouble (Taylor's Version) ~ Taylor Swift

Earned It ~ The Weekend

I See Red ~ Everybody Loves an Outlaw

Into it ~ Chase Atlantic

Lost in the Fire ~ Gesaffelstein, The Weekend

Taste ~ Ari Abdul

Sleepless ~ Dutch Melrose

Take What You Want ~ Post Malone Ozzy Osbourne & Travis Scott

Never Let Me Go ~ Florence + The Machine

All I Wanted ~ Paramore

Shameless ~ Camila Cabella

The Best I Ever Had ~ Limi

Hypnotic ~ Zella Day

You Should See Me In A Crown ~ Billie Eillish

Scars To Your Beautiful ~ Alessia Cara

Panic Room ~ Au/Ra

Head Above Water ~ Avril Lavigne

Never Leave ~ Bailey Zimmerman

I'm Gonna Find You ~ LØCH ANAM

I Did Something Bad ~ Taylor Swift

Survivor ~ Scott Stapp

Prologue

Ten years ago

I sit next to her bed, with tears streaming down my face. Her frail hand is clenched in mine, Jack's position mirroring mine at her other side. I glance up at his face to find the tear stains along his cheeks, and it breaks my heart even more. His dark blue eyes red from tears, his dark hair no longer styled from the way he's been tugging at it while we've been waiting for any news. My big brother has always been the fiercely strong one of the two of us. Always there to rescue me from my pain. This time, we're drowning together.

My best friend, Hadley, has been plastered to my side since we found out about the accident. Never leaving me, even to go to the bathroom. I had to put a stop to her joining me in the stall, making her wait outside. I may be breaking, but damn, I have boundaries.

Only twenty minutes after we made it to the hospital, Hadley and I walked out of the bathroom to find Greyson fucking Mancini standing alongside my brother. Several inches taller than Jack, with dark brown hair and hazel eyes that look gold in the harsh hospital lights, stands my brother's best friend, the object of my infatuation since I was ten.

"Hey, Ry," Greyson's sympathetic tone nearly makes me crumble, and my only response is a nod of acknowledgment. He pulls Hadley in for a side hug and releases her back to me. It doesn't escape my already fragile emotional state that he's never given me that kind of attention. I know Hadley looks at him like a big brother, but damn, what I'd give for a hug right now.

I sniff back the tears and try to put my mask back in place. After our dad left when I was only two, it's just only ever been the three of us. Mom always said *"Batteries have treated me better than any man. I don't need one."* She never dated since the day he left. I have to be strong. I have to get us through this. Someone has to help her through this.

Doctor Rutz comes in to speak with us after an hour.

"Ryan, Jack, I'm sorry to tell you that your mother likely won't make it through the night." He rakes his hand through his hair like he's anxious to share the news we had been dreading. "The injuries to her brain and spinal cord are too severe. She won't wake." He pauses, gripping my shoulder. "I'm so sorry."

He doesn't bother sticking around with us after that, slinking out once he delivers her prognosis.

"No, Jack, she can't leave us. How are we supposed to make it through without her?" A sob wracks through my chest as the words come out. He stands, walking to join me where I'm sitting.

"We just have to, sis." His voice trembles as he says the words.

With Hadley on my right side, Jack on my left, and Greyson looking across my mom's still form, I hear the shrill tone of the machine indicating her heart has stopped beating.

I collapse into my best friend, seeking comfort. I hear a loud crash and crunch a second before Jack's warmth disappears from my other side.

I jolt upright, looking around to see Greyson's fist through a wall. I jump up, crossing the room, taking his hand in mine.

"Grey, what the hell is wrong with you?" The question comes out in a shriek. He doesn't say a word, his hazel eyes meeting mine in a silent conversation. I raise my hand to stroke his face, but he jerks away from me like I've struck him. I drop his hand and move away. "Get that checked, please." I stand and turn back to Hadley, who has an expression of confusion mixed with the heartbreak of my mom's passing. I look back at her body, and the tears start flowing again.

A week later, Jack and I stand together at a graveside service with our closest family and friends, mourning the loss of our mother.

Hadley has been with me every day, never leaving my side. She's held onto me through all the nightmares and tears.

Greyson and Jack have been out drinking nearly every night, stumbling home at all hours. I don't know how well my brother is coping considering how many times they've both come back to our house, barely able to make it through the front door.

Before the service, we found out Mom paid the house off and set enough money aside for both Jack and me to be set for college. Talk about a double-edged fucking sword. I get to live out my dream without my biggest cheerleader, apart from Hadley, in my corner.

The day is a blur of people offering their bullshit condolences. I dissociate about halfway through, not realizing that we are the only ones left until the sun is setting. Hadley holds onto me as I say my final goodbyes. Jack and Greyson follow closely behind us as we make our way to the car.

Two weeks after mom's death, Greyson and Jack stand out in front of our house next to a U-Haul van. I walk up to them from where I parked my car, with panic rising in my chest. The unease causes everything I ate that day to churn in my stomach, ready to make a reappearance no one needed nor wanted to see.

"What's going on, guys?" I ask quietly.

"Greyson is leaving. He got a tattoo apprenticeship in Miami." Jack explains, pausing for a moment, watching for a reaction. "He's leaving now. He was waiting so he could say goodbye to you." My big brother shoves into Greyson's shoulder with a silent admonishment as he walks away.

"Ry," Greyson holds a hand out towards me, which I just glance down at. "I didn't want to tell you until I was sure."

"So, you're sure now. You didn't have to hide that from me, Grey." I reply as a defeated sigh passes my lips. "I'm proud of you. You'll do great!"

"Ry," he pulls me into an embrace for the first time in our lives with a low growl in his chest.

It sends a thrill through my body that I've never experienced before. His masculine scent of sandalwood and juniper invades my senses. After wishing to be this close for five years, he chooses now, moments before he's going to walk out of my life, to touch me. I pull back with tears threatening to break free.

"I can't wait to see how amazing you become." I plaster on a fake smile. "Bye, Grey."

I turn on my heel and run into the house past my brother, who, if looks could kill, would be up on homicide charges right now.

Chapter One

He peels my top off over my head. His warm mouth moves rapidly from my lips to my neck and chest, like he isn't sure where to start. I groan as he pulls the cups of my bra down, exposing my breasts to the cool air, my nipples taut with arousal. With no coaching necessary at this point, he latches his mouth to my right nipple, sucking it between his teeth and biting down to elicit a feral cry in ecstasy at the delicious pain. Heat is rushing to my core, and I'm so ready for this to really get started.

"Fuck yeah, Ryan," he moans, even though I haven't touched him yet. Before I can shut him up with my lips against his, he comes closer to whisper in my ear. "Say something dirty, baby."

As if someone dumps a cold bucket of water over my head, all the arousal I was feeling is gone. The heat turns to ice, and my wells dry up. Leaning into him, I whisper back. "Something dirty." I stand and grab the few pieces of clothes he was able to take off of me and pull them back on.

"Sorry, Jax, we're done here. No hard feelings. Yeah?" I chuckle as I leave the room.

The next morning I wake up deciding I need to forget the previous night's events. Jackson has been nice the few times I've been around him but obviously, that was a mistake to take it further. I grab my phone and send a message in the group chat that is pinned to the top of my messaging app, right above Jack.

Ryan

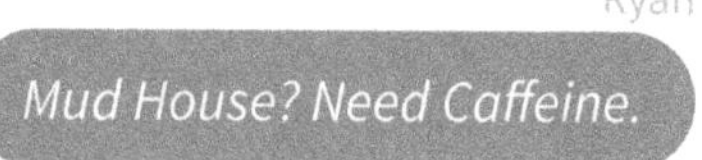

Not awake enough to form full sentences, I flop my head back on my pillow as I wait for a response, which doesn't take long.

Pickle

You gave him a mouth hug, didn't you?

Hadley

Oh. My. God! Say it's not true! Jax?! Of all people! This man has insisted on spending all of his money on strippers for years now!

I shake my head.

Ryan

Don't worry, Moms. I didn't sleep with him. He dried me up before it could even get that far. He got to a solid second base before it ended.

Pickle

You poor thing. You need to get those cobwebs swept out from in there. Are you going to let me do it for you yet?

Hadley

Kat! LOL

Pickle

What? I love Clay and all, but it's not like Ry and I haven't had sex before. I'd bang both of you if you'd let me. My girls are sexy!

Ryan

Obviously I was better than Clay if you're still bringing it up.

I giggle to myself. She's been randomly dropping hints about being with women lately.

Ryan

Can we please meet for coffee, you crazy bitches.

I don't bother waiting for a response. I dress in a hurry; I pull on my favorite navy blue yoga pants that are as soft as butter and a thin-strapped teal crop top. It's unseasonably warm for this time of year, so I'm enjoying showing off the extra skin for a while longer. My flat stomach is on display, the supple skin along the underside of my breasts barely contained. My trusty waterproof hiking boots cover my feet. They don't know it yet, but we're going on a hike to one of my favorite spots for a photoshoot. With my shoulder-length blonde hair styled in beach waves pulled halfway up into a clip with a few rogue tendrils framing my face,

I grab my camera bag and everything else I keep at home for shoots outside of the studio. Once my Jeep is packed, I drive over to Mud House to find Pickle and Hadley hovering around the counter, chatting with our friend, Kayleigh, who just so happens to be the owner.

"Hey, babes!" I call as I walk over towards the girls.

I'm not two steps from them when I hear my name from a familiar voice behind me. "Ryan Elise Sage!" I groan as I turn towards my brother's voice.

"What, Jack?" I roll my eyes at him, "You act as though we didn't just see each other this morning."

"Yeah, I know, but there's something that came up that I wanted to tell you before you found out on your own." His dark blue eyes morph from stern to gentle.

"Oh, cut the shit, big brother. What is it?" I give him my best, *I'll throat punch you,* look. Before another word left his mouth, I heard Hadley squealing behind me.

"GREYSON FREAKING MANCINI! When the hell did you get back into town?" The excitement in her voice would be intoxicating if it weren't my worst nightmare come to life.

The blood drains from my face, and I slowly turn to see him standing with Hadley and Pickle, his arm wrapped around Hadley in a side hug like they used to share when we were younger. I'm in a fever dream. It's the only thing that makes sense at this moment. He'd never come back here.

Time stands still as I take him in. The years sure as hell took care of him. He's even more beautiful than when he left town.

When he left me.

I may have only been a teenager when he left, but I was so in love with that man it wasn't funny, and he knew it. He had to have known it. Everyone else did. Hell, even his high school girlfriend, Raven, threw out snide comments when I was around with my brother, making her frustration with my existence very well known.

My eyes rake up his chiseled frame. Nothing has changed, yet everything has changed. His chest is broader, his arms thicker with muscles that would put a bodybuilder to shame. Every visible inch of skin below his neck is covered in the most gorgeous and intricate artwork I've ever seen. When my eyes finally meet his, the burst of gold from the center fading to a honey brown before settling into an olive green, they steal my breath like always.

"Grey," his name is a whisper, a prayer on my lips.

"Hey, Ry." The corners of his lips twitch into a smug smirk.

Those words from him. His voice, as smooth as velvet, runs bone-deep, awakening a desire in me I long since forgot.

Fuck me.

Chapter Two

The sound of my name on her lips is the sweetest thing I've heard since I left ten years ago. The time I spent hunched over creating art on human canvases holds nothing over the look in her chocolate eyes as she takes me in.

I noticed her the second I walked in. I would have known that body anywhere, even if Jack hadn't been standing with her. She's been ingrained into my mind since she was seventeen. Ry was always Jack's annoying baby sister when we were kids, following us everywhere. We were both protective as hell of her, but it was never more than that.

When she turned seventeen, though, everything changed for me. She blossomed into a woman overnight, but my twenty-two-year-old horny fuckboy self refused to follow that path with her. I was never the same after finding out Raven, my high school girlfriend, cheated on me for most of our relationship. I couldn't use Ryan like that just to scratch an itch. She always meant more to me than that.

"I hope I'm not crashing the party. Jack told me this was the best place for coffee." My eyes never leave hers. The warm chocolate color that still makes my dick twitch anytime I see a fucking Hershey's bar.

"Yeah, our friend Kayleigh owns the place. She makes the best peppermint mocha lattes and muffins you'll ever experience." Hadley chimes in, still excited to see me, completely oblivious to Ryan's internal struggle.

A woman with hair that matches Ry's shirt with a huge rack barely contained by a sundress, walks over with her coffee in hand, wrapping her free arm around Ryan's waist. "Do I have to beg for an introduction, babygirl?" She flicks her long teal hair over her shoulder, waiting and glaring at me.

Babygirl?

I arch a brow at Ryan, who responds, "Pickle, this is Grey." Her eyes are still trained on mine, the brown orbs not breaking contact. "Grey, Pickle. Well, Kat, but I call her Pickle because she hates it, and I think it's adorable. She made the mistake of telling me that was her nickname in college, and well, you know me. I always stick to a bit." She rambles adorably and I fucking love it. Her cheeks tinge in the most perfect shade of pink.

I haven't even been around her for ten minutes, haven't had the pleasure of discovering if she still smells like kiwi and mango. I haven't even touched her, and my dick is already responding to her presence.

Fuck me.

"Nice to meet you, Kat slash Pickle." I smile as I hold out my hand to shake hers. She simply looks at it and nods her head.

"Uh-huh, well, we've got things to do." She pulls Ryan alongside her and yells for Hadley to follow.

Hadley squeezes my side again and whispers to me. "We've all missed you." She smiles up at me with a wink before scurrying out the door.

Fuck, could that have gone any worse?

Jack scowls at me, a fire in his eyes. He's only ever looked like that at the shitheads we used to threaten for trying to hook up with Ryan in school.

"What?" I roll my eyes.

"You know what, asshole. You're just here to settle up, and then you're going back to your beach life." His voice gruff, "Don't fucking lead her on."

"Are you serious? It's Ryan!" I roll my eyes at him. It *is* Ryan. My dick throbs in my pants, reminding me how much of a fucking liar I am. I'm gonna need to keep my distance while I'm here. This will only end in a shit show of hurt feelings.

Several hours later, I step into my childhood home. My dad never could find it in his heart to change anything after mom died. He said it was her home and always would be. Back then, I hated it. The memories blinded me in every space I entered. Now that he's gone, I can feel them both in each room, and it feels somehow gut-wrenching and cathartic simultaneously.

I can't believe they're both gone. Dad and I hadn't seen eye to eye for quite some time. He hated that I took the apprenticeship over the corporate job he lined up for me at his company. He was so angry at me last year when he had to sell the company so he could retire.

"Son, you had your fun. Put your schooling to use and come take over our company. YOUR company."

I couldn't even assign a digit to the number of times I heard that over the last five years. I hadn't spoken to him in a month before I got the call a few days ago. He had a stroke. I was in the middle of working on a sleeve I had been looking forward to when I saw the hospital was calling me. I barely wiped down and bandaged up my client before telling him I'd reschedule and finish for free. Once I picked up Ellie, it only took me ten minutes to take the normally twenty-five-minute drive to the airport and leave on the first flight I could book. He held on until I got to his bedside before he passed. I got to tell him I love him, and that was it. My dad was gone. I called Jack on my way to the hospital from the airport for a place to crash. I don't know if I can stay here. This house holds too many memories.

My phone dings as I stand there, pulling me out of the memories of my past, both distant and recent. I can't help but get lost in them while in this place.

Hadley

> *Hey Buttface! I'm pissed you didn't tell me you were coming home. Let's catch up. So much has happened since you left.*

I chuckle at the memories Hadley stirs with that nickname. She used to give me shit all the time growing up. She hated how protective Jack and I were of the two of them.

Greyson

I'm not sure how long I'm here, but I'll make time for my favorite pain in the ass. I'll text you later, kid.

The image of Ryan comes rushing back to me. Hadley is still as beautiful as ever. She was always a cute kid. But Ryan, damn. She grew up to be a hell of a woman. A body that she displayed proudly, a huge fucking change from the timid girl she once was.

Chapter Three

I walk slowly, my mind racing as we walk towards my Jeep. I toss the keys to Pickle because I know I sure as hell can't drive right now. Fucking Greyson, of all goddamn people. I turn to Hadley, who is in the back seat looking out the window, seemingly oblivious.

"Did you know?" The statement was more accusation than question.

"Know what?" she responds innocently.

"Cut the shit, Had. You know what I'm asking." I glare at her.

"Of course, I didn't know. Though, if I did, I still wouldn't have told you." Her confidence since dating Connor is annoying the shit out of me right now. "You would have run for the hills had you known. You've never gotten over him, and from what I've seen on his social media, he hasn't seriously dated anyone since he moved down there."

I groan. Of course, she's always tried to be my matchmaker with Grey. I cringe at the thought. He was never *my* Grey. He made that clear time and time again when he constantly took on the role of my second big brother. It wasn't until the day he left that he actually touched me. I still feel that hug when I think of him. His warm, strong muscles wrapped so tightly around me. It felt like he didn't want to say goodbye. I tried and failed to find the cologne he wore that day. Just so I could smell him again, so I could pretend he hadn't walked out of my life.

We step out of my Jeep when we arrive at the entrance to the trail we often take on days like this. It's my favorite place to shoot, and with the amazing scenery, I always manage to get great shots of my girls. I grab my camera bag, tripod, and travel reflectors, strapping them to me before we start the trek to the first location. As I get set up for the first spot in a small opening off the trail, I see Hadley texting on her phone. The wicked grin plastered on her face is a clear sign she's talking to Connor. I roll my eyes as I hand Pickle the reflector and pull out my camera. I carefully remove the protective cover from both the camera and lens before connecting it and then removing the lens cap. I take a deep breath, centering myself with the fresh April air.

"Hadley, you're up," I call her over my shoulder as I snap a few shots before checking to ensure the settings are ok with the lighting as it is.

I look up to see her walking towards Pickle. She hands over her phone with a sly grin on her face. I raise a brow at her, and she shrugs her shoulders.

"What did you do?" I ask as she walks into the frame while I snap a few test shots.

"Nothing!" she says too quickly.

I shrug, knowing I won't get any more out of her. Positioning them where I want them, I quickly get to work, wanting to do a few more locations along the trail before the day is done.

The two of them together are so photogenic, it really isn't fair. I've never had a picture of myself that I've liked. My eyes are always closed or I'm making some sort of weird face. The last time we tried to get a selfie, I made them crop me out because it was so bad.

That evening I'm laying on my couch when I get a text message from Hadley.

Hadley

Babe, you look hot.

A photo from this afternoon is attached.

I'm standing a few yards from the camera, looking off into the distance past Hadley, who took the picture, with my camera in my hand partially lifted as If I was about to snap a shot.

My blonde hair is pulled halfway off my face, showcasing my deep brown eyes. My expression is relaxed, beautiful, and thoughtful. One of peace. The yoga pants and tank top hugged my curves so beautifully that I barely recognize myself. The sun in the background illuminates the scene like it's from some romance movie.

I see bubbles as I stare down at my phone, amazed at the shot Hadley was able to get of me. When the next notification comes through, it's not Hadley that's responded.

No, she didn't.

Greyson

God damn, Ry.

Hadley

I know, right, Grey! She's stunning!

I don't even respond. I pull up a different chat and press the button for a group video call.

Pickle and Hadley answer simultaneously.

"WHAT THE FUCK, HADLEY!" I yell into the phone.

"What happened?" Pickle's expression is laced with confusion.

At least she's not in on this betrayal.

"She sent a picture of me to Greyson and started a fucking group chat with the three of us," I whine.

"Hadley, you didn't!" Pickle scolds.

"What? She wasn't going to make a move, and I could see she was paralyzed when she saw him." The amusement on her face is clear. "If you remember, my love, you did something very similar to me, and look how that turned out." She smiles as she pans the camera to Connor, who is on the computer beside her. The smirk he attempts to hide is not so subtle.

"Ladies," Connor says as he winks towards the camera.

"I hate you." I groan.

"No, you don't. Talk to him. You've been in love with him since we were kids. At the very least, catch up with him." Her eyes soften.

My phone buzzes with another notification. I feel my eyes widen as I see the message come through, this time between just the two of us.

Greyson

It was really good seeing you today. It's been too damn long.

"Uh, he–" I stutter. "He, he messaged me."

Hadley is giggling like a maniac who's just won the lottery.

"Babygirl, you do what you feel most comfortable with. I got you, even if Hadley is meddling." Pickle's gentle smile eases my nerves.

"Like she didn't meddle?" Hadley's sass has actually become one of my favorite things since she and Connor started dating, just not when it's directed towards me.

"I love you both, but I'm hanging up now." I don't wait for a response before I disconnect the call.

I lay my phone on my chest and stare at the ceiling, contemplating my next move. My phone vibrates against my chest with another notification, and it takes all my strength not to look at it. Instead, I sit up and pull out my laptop. I retrieve the memory card from my camera and connect it to my computer to upload the pictures I took earlier.

I spend no more than fifteen minutes working on a picture of Pickle and Hadley before my phone vibrates again. Surely, he's not triple-messaging me without a response. I pick up the phone to check my messages.

Greyson

I'm only back for a week or two. It depends on how long it takes to clean out Dad's house and plan the service.

Greyson

I want to see you and catch up before I have to leave.

Greyson

I've missed you, Ry.

What the hell? His dad's service? I pick up the phone, dialing Jack. It rings twice before he answers.

"Why the fuck didn't you tell me about Grey's dad?" I bark at him as soon as I hear his voice.

"Because," he pauses, I hear him walking away from the TV and a door click before he continues. "Your feelings have been clear since you were a kid. I didn't want you to be the one to comfort him, because I know him. It would only end badly for you."

"I'm a grown woman, Jack. That isn't for you to decide." I snarl at him before disconnecting the call. I pull up my messages and give in to my need to respond.

Ryan

I'm so sorry, Grey, I didn't know.

Greyson

It's OK. I figured Jack wouldn't tell you.

Ryan

Do you need help with anything?

Greyson

If you're up for helping me organize the house and get everything ready to sell or put into storage. I'll be there tomorrow morning at eight.

Ryan

Sure, I'll see you then.

Ryan

I've missed you, too.

Chapter Four

Greyson

When Hadley sent me that picture, I nearly busted in my pants. Had I not been in the same room with her brother, I probably would have taken care of myself right then and there.

Her last message hits me like a ton of bricks.

Fuck, if she only knew.

I sit there trying to discreetly look at the picture again while Jack is talking to me about my plans while I'm here. I had every intention of getting in and out, but seeing Ry? I don't know if I can stay for a week without everything changing.

"What do you plan on doing tomorrow?" Jack's question pulls me from my thoughts.

"I'm going to start clearing things out of the house. I need to figure out what I'm getting rid of." I pause before mentioning Ryan.

"I can't get out of work until Wednesday, but I can come by in the afternoon around three-thirty to help." Jack's response has me scrambling for an excuse for him not to come.

"Let me get through the first day, and I'll let you know how much help I need," I grunt.

We spent the rest of the night drinking Corona after Corona, catching up on the past ten years since I left. It's as if no time has passed between us, though I can't help noticing how much Jack has changed. Gone is the carefree guy I once knew. His mom's death and my leaving fucked him up on a level I didn't realize. I feel guilty for that every day, but the opportunity was something I couldn't turn down. Had I chosen differently, I wouldn't own my own shop, having the opportunity to tattoo some incredible people and a few celebrities along the way. My success gained me a large following, keeping my books constantly full.

After a few hours of hanging with Jack, I excuse myself to crash, knowing I have a lot on my plate in the morning.

Her chocolate eyes lock on mine as my cock disappears past the most luscious pink lips I've ever seen, sinking into her mouth. I feel the head brush the back of her throat. She gags around my thick length, making me groan. She doesn't let it deter her from taking me deeper. She digs her nails into my hips as she continues to fuck me with her perfect mouth. I feel my balls tighten as I near the precipice.

My eyes fly open as I feel four feet land hard on my chest.

"Son of a bitch," I curse. "Ellie, what's wrong, sweet girl?" My calico Maine Coon is digging her nails into my chest as she howls. I look over to see her food bowl is half empty. I glance at the clock to see it's only three A.M. I haven't even been asleep for four hours.

Ugh. Moments like this make me question why I got a cat.

I roll out of bed to fill her bowl; she purrs loudly as she rubs against my legs when the bowl is full. Closing the lid on her food container, I climb back into bed and stare at the ceiling. One arm under my head, I close my eyes and see those beautiful eyes staring up at me once more.

Fuck, how am I supposed to sleep now?

I groan, wrapping my hand around my cock, stroking myself while imagining her lips sucking me into her throat like in my dream. Her nails digging into my hips as I forcefully fuck her mouth, tears running down her face as she takes me into her throat, gagging but refusing to slow down, so eager to please me.

I barely last five minutes with my imagination before I find my release. I feel like a teenager seeing his first set of tits again as I grab a tissue from the bedside table to clean myself up. I need to find someone to fuck and get this obsession out of my system. I can't go there with her.

I stare at the ceiling again for hours before I finally succumb to unconsciousness.

My alarm goes off at seven, and I roll onto my side to turn it off, throwing my arm over my face. I groan as Ellie curls up against my chest. I snuggle with my favorite furry girl for a few moments before finally rolling the rest of the way out of bed.

My plan to take a quick shower fails when my thoughts drift to the vivid dream I had last night. I find my hand wrapped around my aching cock again. A firm grip pumping myself with my eyes closed, visions of Ryan bent over in front of me flash behind my closed eyelids. Thrusting inside of her perfect pink pussy. I can feel her walls fluttering around me as her climax nears.

Fuck.

I find my release too soon.

With as many times as I've thought of her over the years, I wouldn't expect that seeing her again would make this infatuation so much worse.

You really need to get some pussy, Grey.

Even my inner voice calling me the name only she uses has me ready to go again.

I pull up to Mud House at seven-forty, hoping I'm not going to be late. I step out of my dad's 1989 Ford Ranger, closing the door behind me before heading towards the cafe. Pulling open the door, I quickly spot who I'm looking for. I walk to the counter like I've done this a hundred times. In truth, I haven't done this since high school.

"Hi, you're Kayleigh, right?" I ask the redhead I met here yesterday.

"Yeah," she smiles brightly at me. "You're friends with Hadley and the girls, right?"

"Yes. My name is Greyson," I smirk down at her. "I was hoping you could help me with something." I pause for a moment, gauging her reaction. "I'm hanging out with Ryan this morning, and I'm not sure what her coffee order is."

"Give me two minutes." She chuckles, shaking her head.

I would have timed her, but I wouldn't have had my stopwatch app ready with how quickly this woman had Ryan's drink, what I ordered yesterday, and a bag that she says is filled with something Ry would appreciate.

I scan my card to pay, and she winks at me as I start to walk away. *What the?*

I come to a halt when I get to my truck and see my ex-girlfriend, Raven, standing next to the driver's side door. I was really hoping to avoid this.

"What do you want, Rave?" I ask, rolling my eyes as I approach.

"I heard you were back in town and wanted to catch up, babe. It's been so long." Her smile makes my stomach turn.

"No thanks, just because I'm back for now doesn't mean that I want anything to do with you." I sigh as I maneuver around her, placing the coffee and pastries Kayleigh insisted on in the car. "In case it wasn't clear when we last saw each other, I'd rather jump into an active volcano than ever be with you again." I brush past her, climbing into the truck. I glance out the window as I back up, her mouth agape. I chuckle to myself at the expression of pure rage etched across her face.

Ten minutes later, I park in the driveway of my childhood home. Ryan sits on the front steps wearing a pair of black bike shorts and a pink cropped t-shirt, a black sports bra peeking out from underneath.

Thank fuck. At least she's wearing a bra today.

She's looking at her phone and doesn't notice me as I open the door, letting myself out.

"Good morning," I pause. "Sorry I'm late, but I had to make a pit stop." I grin at her as I walk over with the coffee outstretched in one hand, holding the bag and my cup in the other.

"How did you-?" she asks as she takes a sip. The soft moan that passes her lips is a direct line to my dick.

"I asked Kayleigh." I clear my throat as I explain, trying to get myself under control. I hand her the bag. "She insisted we have these, too." I shrug.

She eagerly takes the bag, opens it, and smirks when she gets a whiff of the peppermint mocha muffins.

Chapter Five

T hat sneaky bitch. I love her. I open the bag to find my favorite muffin, peppermint mocha. It's like having Christmas all year long. I place my coffee on the step next to me so I can pull out a muffin and hand the bag back to Grey.

"Thank you."

I smile up at him through dark lashes as I take a small bite of the muffin. I can't help the moan that leaves me when the flavors first hit my tongue. It's a perfect medley of chocolate, coffee, and peppermint. I really don't know how she manages to do this every single time. I look up at Grey, his face scrunched up like he's in pain.

"Sure, Ry." His voice is strained.

"Everything ok?" I ask after I've finished chewing.

"Uh," he clears his throat, shaking his head. "Yeah, sorry. Let's go inside. It's cooler."

He holds out his hand to help me stand. I raise my brow at him as I accept the gesture.
"Thanks."

Grey walks in front of me to unlock and open the door. As he passes, I take in his toned, ink-covered legs, encased in red basketball shorts, and the black t-shirt he's wearing that's so tight I'm not sure how it hasn't ripped over his broad chest and thick arms. He steps aside, allowing me to enter ahead of him.

"Wow, your dad really never changed a thing, did he?" I ask, shock in my voice.

"Not a thing," he chuckles. The deep, familiar sound reverberates through me.

I've missed him too much.

I make myself at home, walking in the kitchen to sit down and finish my muffin before we get started for the day. Grey doesn't sit with me. I notice him out of the corner of my eye, leaning against the door frame, arms crossed over his broad chest.

Has he been reading Hadley's romance books?

"How have you been?" The loaded question he drops is like a grenade ready to explode.

"You mean, since you left and didn't bother checking in with any of us?" I don't bother hiding the bitterness.

"Ry, don't be like that. You know why I left." He groans. "I've always just been a phone call or text away. You know that. My number hasn't changed."

"Mine hasn't either," I deadpan.

"Fuck, Ry, really? I told Jack to have you call me when I finally got settled. I hated that I left so quickly." He growls at me.

"You what?" I cut him off before he could continue.

"Nevermind. Let's just get this started." He runs his hand through his hair, something he always did when he was done with a conversation he didn't want to have.

I take a big gulp of my coffee, flinching as it burns my tongue–*coffee's hot, dumbass*– before standing and leaving it on the table. Following him to his dad's room I notice there are boxes and packing supplies in every room we pass. My mind is whirling from the conversation over breakfast.

What did he mean that he asked Jack to have me call him? Jack never said anything to me about that and he knew how hurt I was when Grey left like he did. He wouldn't want to see me enduring the emotional pain I was going through at the loss of him.

We spend the rest of the morning figuring out what needs to get tossed, kept, or donated. He acts like the conversation this morning never happened and I'm not sure if I'm ready to address what was said. I have a list of things on my phone to do, including getting donation items to the domestic violence shelter. While they may not need men's clothes at the shelter we've been working with, they'll be able to get them to the appropriate centers. Either way, there could be a need for beds & bedding for anyone starting over. Any little bit helps.

Since Hadley's survival from Andy, Pickle and I have been helping her support domestic violence survivors as much as we can through the programs we've found near us. I don't know how much of Hadley's story Grey knows, so I don't disclose anything. It's her story to tell, when and if she chooses. I start to take towels and bedding from the linen closet when I feel a hand on my hip as Grey walks up next to me.

"Let's break for lunch. I'll order from the Indian place we like." He grins down at me.

"Uh, they closed a few years ago. There was a robbery that traumatized the owner." I continue pulling out bedding into my arms. "He shot the guy who was attempting to rob them after the guy pointed a gun at his wife."

"What the fuck happened to Central Falls while I was gone? Damn." He pauses, his hand still on my hip. "Anything else you're in the mood for?"

You.

"There's a Thai place that we like to go to. It's by Connor's work." He drops his hand and raises a brow at me. "Let me find the number."

I place the bedding into a box and walk to the kitchen to grab my phone since I left it there when I was done with my muffin. I notice five unread messages I instantly ignore, knowing it's the girls trying to pry. I bring up an internet browser on my screen and type in the restaurant. District Thai. I give him my phone so he can look at the menu.

"Sounds good. I can order, and we can have it delivered, or I can go get it." His voice has an edge that wasn't there a few minutes ago.

"We should probably go get it. Delivery usually takes for-ev-er." I enunciate each syllable to get the point across.

"I can go."

"Why can't I go with you?" I ask, confused by his sudden brusque behavior.

"I mean, you can. Do you want me to take you to see Connor or something while I wait for the food?" His voice comes out tight, laced with frustration.

"Why the hell would I want to see Con? He's a pain in my ass, I love him, but hell no. He'll find something else to pick on me about." I laugh.

"What? Why would he? Why would you be with someone you don't like?" He raises his brow again as he fires question after question at me.

"Are you on crack?" I can't stop the laugh that bubbles from my chest. "Oh my god, that's rich. Connor is *Hadley's* boyfriend. He may be a silver fox, but he's become like an even older brother that I never wanted. I deal with enough from Jack." I sigh.

"Oh," he visibly relaxes.

"Why the hell would you think I was with Connor?" I playfully smack Grey's chest.

"Nevermind. Come on. Let's go." He turns away from me and walks towards the front door.

I follow him out to his dad's old Ranger, climbing into the passenger seat like I used to when Andy, Hadley, Jack, Grey, and I would sneak away during the summer for day trips to the city. Hadley and I would sit up front next to Grey, Jack and Andy sprawled out in the bed of the truck like the heathens they were. I chuckle to myself, lost in memories.

Before I know it, we're pulling up to District Thai. We both exit the truck and meet at the front before heading inside. Ever the gentleman, Grey opens the door for me, allowing me to walk ahead of him.

Deciding to escape the house for a bit longer, we agree to eat here and follow the host to the last booth available, which is usually reserved for a much larger group. The host recognized Grey and immediately told us not to worry and that we could stay as long as we like.

"Just how big is your social media following?" I laugh as the host walks away.

"Eh, I don't pay much attention to the overall number. I'm just concerned about sharing my art with the world." His lips turn up in a lopsided grin that just melts my insides.

"Why don't you tell me what's been going on with you? The ink is a good look for you." I say shyly.

Who am I kidding? You've always looked good.

"Thanks, Ry," he chuckles. "You look pretty damn good too."

Chapter Six

*P*retty damn good doesn't describe how perfect this woman looks.

"Oh my God, are you two on a date?" Hadley squeals from across the restaurant. She and Kat walk towards our table.

I mask my annoyance at them joining us. I may love Hadley like a little sister but I need more time alone with Ryan.

"Pretty sure we've established years ago that he would never. So, no."
Ry's voice is pained as she responds.

"What are you guys doing here?" I ask, ignoring the way Ryan's
comment guts me.

"We came for lunch. Connor is meeting us." Hadley smiles. "Mind if
we join you? I'd love for you to meet him."

I don't say anything, just move around the booth so that I'm next to
Ryan. Kat slides in on Ry's other side, while Hadley settles on my left.

"What happened to Andy?" I ask Hadley as I take a sip of my water.
She visibly tenses.

"Uh, Ryan didn't tell you?" She twists her fingers in her lap while
Ryan shakes her head. I look between them both, confused. Clearly, I've
missed something. "Well. It's a long story." She glances at the door, and
her eyes light up when a man older than me starts walking towards our
table. His brow raises when he sees me next to Hadley.

"I can tell you later," she says softly.

"Mo Ghrá," the older gentleman says with a thick Irish brogue.

*Damn, no wonder Hadley melts into him. I would too with how he looks
on top of that accent.*

"Hi baby," she smiles up at him, scooting closer to me so he can sit next
to her. "This is Greyson, the friend I told you about." She leans into him,
his arm wrapped protectively around her.

"Nice to meet you, I'm Connor." His genuine smile starkly contrasts
his possessive look when he first arrived.

We sit around chatting for hours, the plans of working around my
dad's house long forgotten. I pieced together some parts of Hadley and
Connor's story, but when I went to ask, Ryan squeezed my thigh under
the table as a warning, shaking her head subtly enough that no one else
noticed.

The server places the check on the table, and I go to reach for it. Connor snatches it and pulls it out of my reach.

"My treat for adding testosterone to this group outing." He laughs.

When it's time to sign the credit card receipt, Connor rolls up his sleeves, revealing fresh ink. My eyes immediately lock on the intricate linework. I smirk to myself, knowing the signature of my first mentor anywhere.

"Nat's still tattooing, I see?" I nod at Connor's arm.

"Not as much now. He's been looking to sell, but no one around here is in the position to buy the shop." He shrugs. "He's been tattooing me for years, so he still works me in when he's feeling up to it."

I nod in agreement. That shop has been in Central Falls since I was a kid.

I remember when I first walked into that shop at fifteen with my dad by my side. He signed off on my first piece. A lily, my mom's favorite flower. She would always stop for them any time she came across them when we were out. Up until the day before he died, he took those flowers to her grave every day. A sad smile pulls at my lips.

"Grey?" Ryan's soft voice pulls me from my thoughts, her hand squeezing gently on my thigh again. "You ok?"

"Yeah, just thinking about my parents." My lips twitch, and I wrap an arm around her shoulders, hugging her to my side. "I'm good." I press my lips to her hair, inhaling the same kiwi and mango mixture as before, making my dick twitch in my pants. I clear my throat when I realize everyone is staring at us.

"So, Greyson. I want to get two tattoos. What's the chance you can help me with that while you're here?" Hadley's mischievous grin reminds me so much of when we were kids.

"Oh boy. Hellion Hadley is at it again. What do you want?" I shake my head with a laugh.

"I can tell ya later, I want to cover up some scar tissue." Her smile wavers, and Connor squeezes her even tighter into him.

"Mo Ghrá," he growls.

"It's time, baby. I need to do this, for me." She presses her hand against his chest.

"Let me see what I can do." I wink at her.

We stayed through the dinner rush, just talking and catching up. The girls have only gotten closer over the years, which seems impossible considering they were thick as thieves before I left. On the way back to my place, I drive across Lambert Avenue to see that Alchemy Ink, Nat's shop, is open. I pull into the lot and park the truck in front of the shop.

"Really, you need a new tattoo? Can't you give yourself one at home?" Ryan's sass is like catnip for my dick.

"Relax, Kitten, I'll be five minutes." I roll my eyes at her as I exit the truck and close the door behind me.

Walking towards the front door of Alchemy Ink is like déjà vu. I never thought I'd be back here again. I step through the threshold to find Nat sitting on the couch against the far wall of the waiting area. A sly grin spreads across his face when he sees me.

"Well, I'll be goddamned! If it's not the prodigal son."

"Hey, Nat." My Cheshire grin mirrors his. "It's been a while."

"I'd say. I didn't expect to see you around here after that grand departure." Nat's gruff chuckle fills the room, "What was it you said? 'Suck my dick, old man.'"

"I was an immature asshole. Now, I'm just an asshole." I wink. "I've always respected you, old man."

He grins at me before a somber look passes over his face.

"I'm sorry about your dad, son. I heard this morning." Nat stands from his position on the couch and takes the few steps needed to reach me, pulling me in for a quick hug and a strong pat on the shoulder. "He's become a good friend over the years. The only way I could keep up with your disappearing ass without figuring out how to use a damn computer."

"Thanks," I respond, shifting uncomfortably. I'm not ready to have a conversation about my dad. "Listen, I wanted to ask you something." I smirk at him.

"And here I thought, after all this time, you just wanted to catch up." He laughs. "What is it, son?"

Chapter Seven

I pull my knees up to my chest and grab my phone from my purse. Opening the group chat I press the video call button.

Hadley answers, holding the phone further from her face than I am, showing she and Pickle are still together.

"He just called me Kitten." I stare at the screen. "Why did he just call me Kitten?"

Hadley is giggling uncontrollably and walks away from the phone while Pickle continues smiling at me through the screen.

"Babe, I think Hadley may be onto something here." Her lips twitch into a smirk.

"Oh, God. Not you, too!" I groan, rubbing my free hand over my face.

"Where are you?" Hadley walks back into the frame with a huge smile plastered across her face that would give the Joker reason to pause.

"I'm in his truck. He stopped by Nat's shop for something." I take a deep breath. "I made a smart-ass comment asking if he really needed a new tattoo, and he told me to *"Relax, Kitten."* I make air quotes with my hand as I explain what he said.

I begin to tell them he's been in there longer than the five minutes he said he'd be when the door to the shop opens, and he exits, sauntering towards the truck.

"He's coming," I say to them, but my gaze is locked on his approaching form. The smile on his face is infectious.

They say something, but I don't hear it. The driver's side door opens, and I look him over with a questioning stare.

"What did you do?" I ask.

"Who are you talking to?" he replies, leaning over to see my screen. Hadley is waving back to him, and Pickle is just sitting there with an unimpressed look. I love how protective that girl is.

"Hey, buttface!" Hadley calls through the phone.

"Cool it with the buttface, or I won't tell you what I just did for you." He waggles his eyebrows at her. She immediately quiets, waiting impatiently for him to continue. "I could have, possibly, just talked to Nat about letting me hold a guest spot at his shop for the next few weeks."

"Weeks?" I gasp. He nods at me with a wink.

"We'll get together for lunch, and you can tell me your ideas for what you want, Hellion." He pauses for a moment, "You too, Pickle, whatever you want." He moves back to the driver's seat and starts the truck. Putting his arm behind my shoulders, he twists to look out the rear window, since this old truck doesn't have a rearview mirror anymore. He backs the truck up and pulls off into the street. My eyes widen when he doesn't move his arm and starts lightly drawing circles onto my neck with his thumb.

"Sounds good! Text me when you get a chance, and we can set a lunch date for the three of us! Bye, Ry!" Her cheesy-ass grin makes me want to throw my phone, but she disconnects the call before I can tell her she's a jackass.

I relax into the seat as Grey continues lightly stroking my skin, unsure exactly what his touches mean.

"Since it's later than we planned, why don't I drop you off, and I can pick you up in the morning." His voice is gentle. "We can grab breakfast, and I'll drive you back to Dad's. You can get your car tomorrow."

"That's fine. I don't have a shoot until Thursday, anyway." I breathe out a sigh of relief.

The sky turned dark while I was waiting for him at the tattoo shop, and I hadn't been able to drive in the dark since Mom's accident. It was so early in the morning the sun hadn't come up, not that it had later in the day, as the rain had been steady for days leading up to the accident. She was on a back road with no street lights and couldn't see the herd of deer on the road until it was too late.

After another ten minutes of driving through our town, Grey approaches my place. I smile to myself, his fingers still caressing the base of my neck.

"Thank you. I'd invite you in, but I need to edit a few things tonight." I smile, the lie flowing so easily past my lips. I'm not sure where he's going with his sudden interest, but I've got to protect myself. I open the door, and he squeezes the back of my neck possessively for just a moment before releasing me so I can slide out.

"Night, Kitten," he winks as I close the door, turning my back to him and walking towards my door. I don't hear the truck pull away until I'm inside with the door closed and locked behind me.

What the fuck.

The birds are chirping too loudly for the middle of April, and I can't help but think, in my semi-conscious state, they shouldn't be back this far north yet. Prying my eyes open, I see flashes of light shining through my bedroom curtains. I roll over, groaning as I grab my phone to see the time. It is only five forty-five A.M. I roll onto my back, staring at the ceiling, thinking about yesterday. It was so weird, Grey giving me little bits of attention I so desperately craved when I was younger. My feelings have never faded, but knowing he's only here for a limited amount of time has my stomach in knots.

Weeks.

The memory of last night filters through my mind. He said he would be here for a few weeks. My mind whirls with the possibility that he could be staying longer *for me*. I shake my head, trying to toss the thought out the window. There's no way he could be staying for me. He's doing Hadley a favor. He's always adored her. It only makes sense that he'd ensure he could give her the tattoo she asked for. If only he knew the reason behind it, why she wants her first tattoos now.

After a few long moments, I moan in frustration and climb out of bed. I walk to my kitchen and pull out a bag of coffee from the cabinet. Filling a filter with enough grounds to make Lorelai Gilmore proud, I place the filter in the basket and put it into the machine. Having already filled the reservoir with water, I place the empty pot under the machine and press start. I sit staring at the rich, dark liquid as it trickles into the carafe. I close my eyes, inhaling the delectable aroma that fills the room. The bold, nutty scents infiltrate my senses as I pour the heavenly drink into my favorite Gilmore Girls mug.

I take my time enjoying my coffee before heading to the bathroom to shower. I pull my nightshirt off over my head and peel my lace cheeky boyshorts past my hips and down my legs before they land on the floor between my feet. I pick them up along with my shirt and place them in the hamper. Stepping into the shower, I stand under the steaming water for a few moments, enjoying the heat seeping into my skin. I close my eyes as the water caresses my skin. I imagine Grey's hands on me as I glide my fingers over my body, pinching my nipples so tightly, the pain sending a jolt of need straight to my core. My right-hand travels down my taut stomach to my pussy, lightly grazing my clit. I gasp at the contact. I continue teasing my nipples with my other hand, alternating back and forth between them. I open my eyes to locate the suction cup dildo I keep in a cabinet next to my shower. Opening the curtain to rummage through the cabinet, I find my trusty toy.

I plunge it against the wall at the perfect height for me to back onto it. I close my eyes again, imagining Grey standing behind me with his hands gripping my hips as I back up to the toy, gently parting my entrance before I thrust back until it's fully seated inside me. Crying out at the intrusion, allowing myself a moment to adjust since it's been a couple of days since I felt the need to reach this type of release. I find a rhythm quickly that sends heat through me, my hand between my legs caressing my clit, applying the perfect amount of pressure. I continue fucking myself with my toy, sliding back and forth on the silicone cock. I find my release twice in a row as I continue fucking myself through the climax.

Sated, I stand tall, cleaning myself and the length of the toy before turning off the shower. I grab a towel hanging from the wall, wrapping it around my hair before pulling the second one off the rack and drying myself before exiting. Securing the towel around myself before walking across the hall to my room. I grab a pair of teal floral yoga pants and a white cropped t-shirt from my dresser. Once the towel is loosened from my hair, I squeeze the excess water droplets before tossing it into the hamper next to my closet. I pull the shirt over my head, forgoing a bra, my damp hair lying across my shoulders. I toss the pants onto my bed and walk back to the dresser, pulling out a white lace thong. I finish getting dressed just as I hear a knock on the door. I rush out to open it, finding Grey there with two cups of coffee in hand. His lips twitch into a lopsided grin as he holds out one cup towards me.

"Oh, hello, beautiful," I giggle as I grab the cup from him.

Chapter Eight

"**O**h, hello, beautiful," she giggles as she takes her cup from my hand, the sound going straight to my dick.

"Usually, I don't like being called beautiful, but from you, I'll make an exception." I wink at her.

"I thought it was obvious, I was talking to the coffee." She shakes her head, laughing at my response.

"Can I come in for a minute before we head out? I need to use the facilities."

She steps aside, allowing me into her home. I look around and see a large sectional with a fleece throw and so many pillows covering the surface I'm not sure where the cushions begin or end. Photographs cover her walls; some of her mom, some of Jack, a lot of the girls. My lips twitch when I notice there are no pictures of any men apart from her brother. The thought quickly turns sour, though, when I realize there are also no pictures of me. Although, I guess I only have one person to blame for that.

Way to go, asshole.

"It's down the hallway to the left," she says, dragging me from my thoughts.

I nod and place my cup on the coffee table in front of her couch. I stride down the hallway to the bathroom, stepping inside and closing the door. I empty my bladder while taking in my surroundings. I do a double-take when I notice something through the partially opened curtain, very bright and purple attached to the shower wall.

"Fuck, Ry," I groan as I tuck myself away, attempting to avoid the aching need growing even more apparent. I hear her footsteps approaching.

"Is everything ok?" The panic in her voice startles something inside me that I'm not quite prepared for.

"Yeah, Kitten. I just saw something I wasn't expecting." I wink at her as I slip past her into the hall.

I hear a gasp and an audible pop as she disconnects the dildo from the shower wall. I chuckle, picking up my coffee from the table as she approaches. Her face is tinged a bright red with embarrassment.

"You ready to go?" I smirk at her. She doesn't speak. She walks past me, grabs her coffee, and walks out the front door. I follow past her and my lips twitch into a flirtatious grin as I watch her lock her door. Her eyes flick up to meet my gaze.

"Stop looking at me like that. I'm not a kid anymore. Of course, I masturbate. Don't try to tell me you don't." She rushes the words out, her embarrassment has turned into a defensive sass.

"Oh, I definitely do. Multiple times a day since I've been back in town." I grab her wrist and tug her into my chest. "You have nothing to be embarrassed about, Kitten. My reaction was because I never pictured you to be a purple toy kind of girl." Her sweet scent fills my senses from having her so close.

"What do you mean? What color did you-" she cuts herself off. "You know what, never mind. I'm already embarrassed enough. We don't need to go there."

She tries to pull away from my grasp, but I don't release her, instead lowering my head so my lips are right next to her ear before I whisper, "I always pictured blue, since it's my favorite color."

She gasps and freezes in my hold. I grin against her ear before releasing her. "Time to go, Kitten. We have things to get done today."

Once we're back at my dad's house, Ryan goes to where she left off yesterday without saying a word. I follow her to the linen closet and move the box closer to her, before I head to Dad's room and start clearing out his things. I spend an hour going through the things in his dresser. I open his closet, a flood of memories crashing into me. I didn't realize

Dad kept most of Mom's wardrobe; even her wedding dress still hung on the back of the closet door. I find her favorite sweater and take it from the hanger it's been placed on for I don't even know how long. I hug it to my chest. I think about her all the damn time, my heart aching for her to see what I've done with my life. I hated everything about this place since we found out she was sick with a brain tumor. A fucking brain tumor took out my mom when she was only thirty-six. She'd been complaining of headaches for months and refused to get checked out. She was always too busy helping Dad at the business or trekking back and forth to get me to soccer practice and games. It was a week before my fifteenth birthday. I was at a game when the police showed up to take me to the hospital. She collapsed while with my dad and had to be rushed to the ER by ambulance. There was nothing they could do. Once they found the tumor, they saw it was taking over the entire frontal cortex of her brain. She never regained consciousness, coding only ten and a half hours after arriving. I would give anything to see her again. To feel her arms around me. She always gave the best hugs.

I feel a hand rest gently against my back and jerk away. I look behind me to see Ryan standing there with a concerned expression plastered on her face.

"Grey?" she whispers. "I called for you but didn't get a response. What's this?"

The question passes her lips as she looks into the closet and sees what I've been lost in for how long? A minute? An hour?

"Oh, Grey." She wraps her arms around my torso, pressing her cheek against my back.

I wipe my face when I realize tears are freefalling from my eyes. "I'm ok, beautiful. I just didn't realize how much of mom's stuff he kept in here. I always thought he got rid of her clothes." I take a deep breath. "It's like I'm saying goodbye to her all over again." I unconsciously press my hand against my pec that displays the first tattoo I got, an in memoriam for my mom.

"Why are you holding your chest like that?" She gasps, jerking away from me. "Are you ok?" The worry in her voice sends a thrill to my dick, which needs to take a damn chill pill. It's not the time.

"I didn't even realize I did that." I offer a small smile. "It's the tattoo I got for Mom. I guess I hold my chest when I think of her." I turn around and pull her into me, relishing the closeness I so desperately need at the moment.

Chapter Nine

His arms wrap tightly around me, giving me a sense of safety and contentment I've never felt before. The people I dated since he left could never have me feeling this way. Yet, I'm supposed to be comforting him. I melt into his embrace, losing myself in the what-ifs his scent elicits. The sandalwood and juniper that are distinctly Grey meld together, reminding me that I've never been able to quite match his signature smell, no matter how many candles and lotions I've bought. I pull away before I can sink any deeper into the memories he stirs inside me.

"Grey." My voice is merely a whisper. "Let's finish this room tomorrow. We can work on the kitchen, instead.

I grab his hand, linking our fingers, and his lips twitch into a smirk at the intimate connection. I lead him out to the kitchen, and we start working together silently. We clear out a lot of items, things his dad held onto after his mom's death, plus things he accumulated in the years since. Grey does insist that we keep a few things, like his mom's Kitchen Aid mixer and a random cake pan, but everything else will be donated. It really makes my job easy and we have everything packed within the hour. I order lunch when we are done and continue into the living room with him while we wait for our food.

"Have you decided what you're getting?" Grey's voice breaks through the sounds of Disturbed's "You're Mine" coming from the Bluetooth speaker.

"What I'm getting?" I stop what I'm doing to turn to him, raising a brow.

"Ink. When I take care of Hellion and Pickle." He chuckles at Pickle's nickname.

"I wasn't planning on getting anything. I thought it was just for them." I stutter.

The truth is, I'd been thinking about getting a tattoo for a long time, but just couldn't bring myself to take the leap. There's only one person I trust to alter my body in such a permanent way, and now, he's standing before me, asking for a chance to do exactly that.

"Of course not, whatever you want. You got it." His smile is sweet as he raises his hand to graze my cheek, brushing a strand of hair from my eyes and tucking it behind my ear.

"Ok." I respond without giving an actual answer. I'm not quite sure how to tell him why I've waited, but I know it's going to come up when I tell him what I want.

Thursday morning has come so quickly that I'm scrambling to get my gear in the car. My client requested multiple locations, so I'm meeting them at the first one. Hopping out of my Jeep, I walk up to find a beautiful human with long dark hair and a slim figure; however, all her beauty disappears the moment she turns around, and I see that it's Raven, Grey's high school girlfriend. This woman made my life a living hell in high school whenever the opportunity arose. It should be illegal that she's as gorgeous as she is. Raven's been going from man to man since they graduated and Grey left, making sure that the next one she ends up with has more money than the last.

Fucking gold digger.

"Raven, I didn't realize you were the one who was scheduled today." I stare at her, my expression blank. I've become a pro at masking my distaste for people since I have to communicate with some vain specimens on a fairly regular basis due to my profession.

"Oh, Ry, don't worry, sweetheart. It will be fun." Her fake giggle makes all the more sense when an older man in a Gucci suit appears from the other side of the Bently she is leaning against. "My man wants to get some fun shots of me, and I knew you would be perfect for what we were looking to do!"

"You're wanting to do a boudoir shoot? And you thought I'd be the best person to do that for you?" I deadpan.

"Of course! You're like my little sister! Remember I used to date your brother's best friend, babe!"

I choke on a laugh. "No, *babe*. What I remember is you making my and my best friend's lives a living hell because you thought we were pathetic," I snarl at her. "So, *babe*. I kindly will be canceling the contract for this shoot since you obviously knew I wouldn't be interested, seeing as you put down your boyfriend's name on the form."

I turn on my heel and climb back into my car, taking just a moment to breathe before speeding out of the lot. I'm so angry at Raven for trying to manipulate me into doing something for her that I don't realize I've already made it to Mud House, driving on autopilot. *Smart, Ryan, real smart.* I pull out my phone and send a text to the girls.

Ryan

You'll never guess who tried to pull one over on me and get me to do a damn boudoir shoot.

Hadley

Was it Grey? Because that would be hot.

Pickle

Oh, tell me you saw his junk. Is he packing?

Ryan

It was fucking Raven! She put her boyfriend's name down for the contract.

Hadley

Oh shit, where are you?

Ryan

> *Mud House. I just got here.*

Pickle

> *I'm leaving the gym now, I'll pick up Hadley on the way.*

I love my friends. We will drop whatever we're doing to be there for one another at a moment's notice, and I couldn't imagine my life without them.

I walk into the coffee shop and order my drink from Jill, the manager of this location. She is usually only here a couple of days a week, so that Jill has coverage for her days off, but I think Kayleigh just uses it as an excuse to visit us. I pull out my phone to send another message while I wait for the girls.

Ryan

> *In case I didn't tell you before, I never liked Raven. I like her even less now.*

Grey

> *What did she do now? *facepalm emoji**

Ryan

> *The manipulation tactics have only gotten worse with her. *eye roll emoji**

Grey

> *Where are you?*

Ryan

> *Mud House, I'm waiting for the girls. Why?*

I look up to see Hadley and Pickle walking towards me from the front door.

"What. The. Fuck." Hadley enunciates each word.

"Exactly." I sigh.

"Hold that thought, I'm ordering us coffee, then you're telling us everything." Pickle winks at me as she walks away. I laugh as I take a seat next to Hadley and rest my head against her shoulder, watching Pickle as she orders their drinks. It only takes a few moments before she sits down, passing Hadley her coffee.

"Ok, spill it, sister." She takes a generous sip of her drink while I go into the details of my morning.

When I finally finish all the gory details, I hear a sharp intake of breath from Pickle as she looks over my shoulder.

"What?" I ask as I look behind me to see Grey standing in the door frame, looking like he's about to rip someone's head off.

Damn.

Chapter Ten

When I read the messages that Raven tried to start shit with Ry, I nearly lost it. After all the things she pulled in high school, I really thought she'd have grown up by now, but apparently not. I tried to keep Raven away from Ryan and Hadley because I knew she was a bitch to both, but more so Ryan. She was incredibly shy when she was younger and Raven used that against her. She's grown out of it since her mom passed away, and from following her social media accounts *which I shamelessly stalked after I left*, I've seen the confident woman she's grown into.

Raven trying to manipulate her has me seeing red. I left Jack at my dad's house packing up tools and ended up here, at Mud House after she texted me. I pull the door open and rush in. My face must show the rage I'm feeling because Kat blanches when she sees me. Ryan turns to meet my gaze, concern etched on her face. She slips off her chair and walks towards me, my dick responding the moment I see her beautiful face.

"Grey?" She reaches for my hand before continuing, "What's wrong?"

"What exactly did she say to you?" I snarl, "I may not have protected you like I should have from her before, but I'll be damned if I allow her to hurt you again." My jaw tenses as I wait for a response.

"Really? That's why you're here?" A sweet smile pulls at her lips. "Grey, I handled it. I'm not a kid anymore. I stood up for myself, for today, and for all the bullshit she pulled in the past. I'm ok." She shakes her head as a soft giggle escapes her.

"I'm sorry I didn't do better back then." I sigh, "I've never forgiven myself for how she treated you." I raise my hand, brushing my fingers against her cheek. She leans into my hand so slightly that I'm not sure if I imagined it until her eyes meet mine again.

"I'm ok, I promise." Her voice is so quiet as she continues staring into my eyes. "Do you want to have coffee with us or do you need to get back to Jack, since I'm assuming you disappeared on him while he was packing something at the house to come here." She chuckles teasingly which makes my already hard dick twitch in my pants.

"I'll stick around for a cup of coffee. We can talk about your tattoos since you're all here." I wink at her. She shrugs as she takes my hand and guides me to their table.

"Fancy seeing you here Buttface." Hadley smiles at me as we approach.

Ignoring her taunt, I take a seat next to Ryan, across from Hadley and Pickle.

"Hi to you, too, Hellion," I respond.

Once I get settled into my chair, I look at Hadley. "So, what kind of ink do you want to get?" Ryan tenses next to me and Hadley's smile turns sad.

"Well, I want to cover up some scarring," she says quietly as she pushes up her sleeves to reveal angry red lines along her wrists.

"What the fuck, Hellion," I growl. "Are you ok? The fuck happened?" Ryan squeezes my thigh under the table to bring me back down.

Hadley's eyes glisten with unshed tears as she goes into the details of the abuse she endured at Andy's hands. I clench my fists under the table as rage cascades through me, and it isn't until she tells me how he died that I start to calm down.

"I wish I had known, Hellion." I gently clasp her hands between mine. "I would have been here for you. I would have killed the motherfucker myself."

Her smile returns at my comment.

"It's ok, My girls and Connor helped me through it." She squeezes my hands before continuing. "Connor has been my anchor through so much of this. I want to honor that. Even if we aren't forever. Which, don't get me wrong," she giggles, "he tells me every day that we are. I want to do this to show not only our strength together, but mine on my own, too."

Kat is tearing up holding Hadley in her arms as she explains what she was hoping to do with her tattoos. I turn her hands in mine, running my fingers over the length of her scars, images running through my mind of ideas for her. I can't wait to help my Hellion take back her power.

When I get back to the house, Jack is finished with the garage. I walk up to him, handing over a Corona from the twelve pack I picked up on the way back.

"Where the hell did you run off to, dick?" he groans as he pops the cap off the bottle.

"Raven is causing problems already." I groan as I pop the top off my own bottle and take a long pull.

"It's fine," I say before I allow him time to ask what happened.

My feelings for his sister need to get in check before he finds out and kicks my ass.

"Let's call it a day. I want to go out," I announce.

I just need to fuck someone, *anyone*, tonight. That will get this need to take Ryan every fucking time I see her out of my system. Hopefully.

"Like you did much of anything today, anyway," he chuckles and shoves my shoulder.

Twenty minutes later we're at the bar, seeing the same crowd we used to before I moved. We're all just older now. It's like a goddamn high school reunion.

I spot a woman I've never seen before; tall, slim waist, perky little tits held up in a poor excuse for a dress. She's hot as hell. Her brown hair sprinkled with pink highlights, it makes her icy blue eyes pop. I nod to

Jack before I walk towards the bombshell at the bar. I take a seat next to her, glancing between her and the bartender until her eyes meet mine. She raises a perfectly shaped eyebrow at me.

"I was just trying to buy a drink here, but you're very distracting." I wink at her.

"Does that really work for you?" she asks, chuckling at me.

"You tell me?" I smile at her and hold out a hand, introducing myself. "I'm Greyson." She's even more attractive up close, but my brain can't stop itself from comparing her to Ryan's effortless beauty. A smile spreads across her face, and as alluring as it is, it's not the smile I want to see.

"Anya," she answers. "And you're cute. Does that line really work, Greyson?"

I chuckle and lean in, close enough to speak low in her ear. "You tell me?" I breathe in her floral perfume before pulling back, grazing her cheek with my fingers and throwing her a wink.

Her cheeks flush with a light shade of pink, "I think it could." She raises her hand and grazes her nails down my shirt over my chest.

Before I came back here, I would be laying on the charm so thick she'd never be able to resist. Now, though, my dick has no interest and I know the damn reason is currently at her place, probably watching some true crime documentary and debating with Hadley on who could get away with murder between the two of them. Now the three of them, if Pickle is into that kind of thing.

"But, I'm," she pauses as she searches for the word, "involved."

"That's probably for the best. My best friend over there is already staring daggers into my head because his sister is in love with me and I'm over here with you." My smile doesn't quite meet my eyes.

She stares at me for a moment before leaning in close, her soft words meant only for me. "Does he know that you're in love with her, too?"

Chapter Eleven

My eyes open and I realize I fell asleep with Pickle on Connor's couch. I attempt to roll over when I realize Pickle is curled up behind me, her arms wrapped around my body, holding me close to her. I find it comical that whenever we end up crashing at each other's houses she always ends up cuddled into one of us. I peel her arms off of my stomach and sit up, stretching my limbs and waking my muscles.

I grab my phone from the table next to me to see the time. It's only eight in the morning so we still have a few hours before we need to be at the shop with Grey. As though he can sense that I have my phone in hand, a text notification lights up my screen.

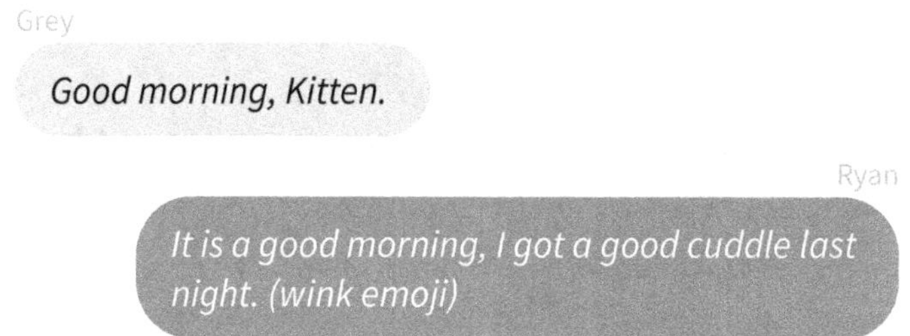

I barely release the giggle that my taunting him is causing me when another text comes through almost immediately.

I can't help but taunt him with my response.

I chuckle to myself and roll my eyes knowing damn well this man doesn't get jealous. The number of times Raven screwed around on him, he didn't bat an eye. I look back down at my phone when my ringtone sounds.

He's calling me? What?

I swipe the answer button and bring the phone to my ear.

"Ryan," Grey growls through the phone before I can say hello. "Who the fuck were you with last night?"

Usually the possessive thing is a major turn off but I've always loved it with Grey since we were younger. Heat pools in my core.

"Why?" I giggle taunting him.

"Ryan." The growl has me weak in the knees this time.

"Are you worried you have some competition, Daddy?" I sass, giving him a moment to stew before I continue pushing my luck.

"I fell asleep on the couch with Pickle. She's a snuggler," I explain as I hear Hadley's loud moan coming from the back of the house.

"Where the fuck are you, Ryan?" His thundering voice rings through the phone so loudly Pickle startles awake.

"What's happening?" Pickle whispers as she sits up beside me. I smile at her and point towards the back of the house and she giggles.

"Ryan, don't make me ask you again. I will take you over my knee and turn your ass red," Grey warns.

I squirm on the couch next to Pickle who is looking at me with a raised brow. "We're at Hadley's. She and Connor must be having a good morning," I giggle into the phone, pausing before taunting him again, "But, you're welcome to spank me whenever you want, Daddy."

"Damn, Ryan," Pickle whispers next to me as she acts like she's fanning herself from my conversation with Grey.

"Fuck, Ry," Grey groans through the phone. "I might just take you up on that, soon."

I smirk at Pickle, not responding to Grey for a long moment when he breaks the silence. "Do you want me to come get you two so you don't have to listen to Hadley?"

"We've heard it plenty of times since they've been together. Honestly, it's kind of hot. Gives me material for later." My laugh is met with another sinful growl.

"I'll see you soon." Grey disconnects the call.

A few hours later, we're walking into Alchemy Ink. Grey is leaning against the wall talking to Nat. A bell chimes when I push open the door, Hadley and Pickle right behind me. Grey turns to look over as we enter. His eyes meet mine with a devilish glint. He says something to Nat who chuckles and walks away.

"You ready, Hellion?" Grey greets us by only acknowledging Hadley.

"Hell yes! Let's do this!" She squeals as she follows behind him.

"Grey," I call after him. "Do you mind if I take pictures while you work?"

He pauses, motioning for the girls to go into the room where he's working. He wraps an arm around my waist, pulling me in close, pressing his lips to my ear. "Only if I get pictures after I redden your ass for this morning, Kitten."

I melt into him, shivering at the suggestion. "Yes, Daddy." The response passes my lips before I realize what I've said. He lightly smacks my ass with the other hand before releasing me to join the others.

I walk in to find Hadley in tears holding up a sketch Grey has drawn for her.

"Buttface!" She sobs as she runs past me and wraps her arms around his waist. "It's perfect!"

She releases him to show me the beautifully detailed Dara knot. It's similar to what I've seen on Connor's bicep, but more feminine, with beautiful baby dandelions weaving through. Their fluffy petals flowing into the wind. They quickly became one of Hadley's favorite flowers since she came through the events with Andy stronger than she was before. Where most of us see a weed, she sees a flower meaning strength and resilience.

Once he's set up, Grey gets to work on Hadley's tattoos, and I begin snapping away, documenting his process and progress. By the time Hadley's done she's got tears in her eyes.

"This was so cathartic," she announces as she stands up, stretching.

It's been a little over three hours. We all walk out to the lobby and grab a snack while Grey cleans up and gets ready for Pickle's ink, which she asked that Hadley and I sit out for. Considering Pickle wants whatever she's getting on her pelvic bone I don't really mind not being there for that. We may have had a thing a few years ago, but seeing her exposed like that would be awkward.

After an hour, Pickle walks towards us in the lobby with a pained smile on her face.

"Are you ok?" I ask as she reaches us.

Hadley and I stand from where we'd been chatting on the couch, pulling her into us.

"Oh, I'm fine." Her smile brightens a little. "Just realized something. I'll tell you guys soon."

Hadley and I exchange looks of concern. Knowing not to push Pickle right now, we drop it and she and Hadley start wandering around the lobby looking at the art Nat has covering the walls.

"Alright, Ry, you're up," Grey calls several minutes later.

I walk back to the room and lean against the doorframe until he acknowledges my presence.

"So, Kitten, are you ready?" Greyson asks, turning his back toward me as he fills the ink caps with the colors we discussed previously.

Our prior conversation about what I want flashes through my mind.

"I want to honor Mom," I pause. "I'd like a cardinal feather, and off-center to that, I'd like an infinity symbol that breaks and makes a heart with her last heartbeat recorded from the EKG machine before she died."

"Shit, that's deep but beautiful. I'd be honored."

"Absolutely." I smile as I peel my shirt over my head, exposing my torso. The blue lace bra I'm wearing-his favorite color-just barely contains my breasts.

"What are you thinking for placement?" He asks as he turns back towards me. "Fucking hell, Ry."

"My ribs." I grin at him as I lay down on the table.

"You're going to be the fucking death of me," he growls.

I smirk, taking pride in knowing I have an effect on him.

It takes him another three hours to finish my piece. By the time he finishes, my skin is on fire. Surprisingly though, not from the tattoo, but his touch. I can still feel the blaze of his fingers against my flesh as I stand, hopping off the opposite side of the table from where he's seated.

"What made you decide to do this now?" he asks as he wipes down his workstation.

Our eyes lock across the table. I take a moment to steel my nerves before answering.

"You weren't the first I wanted you to be, so this was the next best thing." Even with our recent flirtation my boldness still takes me by surprise.

"Ry." His response is a whisper; he stands, and I worry he's going to walk out. He's been so hot and cold, but earlier, I didn't imagine that smack on my ass, did I? He leaps over the table like a fucking gazelle and his mouth crashes against mine, all in the same breath.

Chapter Twelve

The feel of her lips against mine causes an eruption of heat to flare inside me. My tongue swipes against her bottom lip, still swollen from where she'd been chewing it earlier, prompting her to open to me. The taste of her peppermint mocha coffee still lingers on her tongue as mine tangles around hers. My arms wrap around her body, holding her firm against my chest. My cock has been straining against my zipper since I turned around to find her with her shirt off, the blue lace bra barely concealing a thing. The way her chest would rise with each breath, pressing her peaked nipples harder against the fabric as she softly moaned while I was applying the ink to her body, had me ready to come in my pants.

I grip her ass, lifting her onto the table, breaking our kiss only to softly speak into her ear. "I need to taste you." Her eyes light up and she nods. "Words, Kitten. Use your words."

"Yes," she whimpers. I hook my fingers into the waistband of her yoga pants and peel them down her body exposing a pair of blue lace boy shorts matching her bra.

"Fucking christ, Ry." I groan as I lean in, pressing my mouth against hers once more before I explore every inch of her body with my lips.

I press kisses against her cheek and down her neck, sucking gently on the pulse point. My hands caress her beautiful, pale skin. When my mouth reaches her full, perky tits, I pull her nipple between my lips through the lace material, sucking hard enough to elicit a breathy moan.

"Grey, please," she begs as her fingers rake through my hair.

With a wicked smile I continue my journey down her body pressing light kisses along her taut stomach. I nip at her pelvic bone before sliding my hands under her ass again, pulling her to the edge of the table, her legs falling open for me. I press my face against her lace covered pussy, inhaling her sweet scent. I run my tongue along her mound and she shudders, another soft moan escaping her lips.

I hook my fingers under the band of her blue little boy shorts, slowly pulling them over her hips and down her legs, exposing her perfectly pink pussy. It's even more beautiful than my imagination could ever conjure. I stare up at her, our eyes meeting as I lower my face back between her legs, inhaling once more before plunging my tongue between her lips. I groan into her as the sweet tangy flavor bursts on my tongue. The delicious little cry that passes her lips at the connection sends me into a frenzy. I lift her thighs over my shoulders while I feast on a meal I've been craving for years. I savor her taste, my tongue lapping up her arousal in languid strokes.

"Grey!" She cries out my name like a prayer to the heavens above. I've never been a man of faith but she could make me a believer.

"Quiet, Kitten," I scold, pulling away briefly, pressing gentle kisses to her clit between each word. "We. Don't. Want. Anyone. To. Hear. Us." I suck her clit between my lips as the last word leaves my mouth and slowly slide a thick finger inside her tight pussy. The sharp gasp when she feels me enter her is music to my ears. I continue devouring her, my tongue swirling around her clit as my finger pumps in and out of her, fucking her tight channel. I feel her tightening around my digit as I pull her clit tight between my lips. She detonates around me, her body shaking as the orgasm takes over. She softly whimpers, remembering my instructions.

I stand and press my lips back against hers, swiping my tongue inside her mouth so she can taste her sweet release. She groans into me. "You did so well, Ry." I smirk at her as I wrap my hand around her throat. "Are you on any birth control?"

"Yes, I have an implant. I haven't been with anyone in over a year." She whispers the confession so low I barely hear it.

My smirk becomes devilish. "Let's see if you can keep quiet while I fill you with my come. Turn around." I release my grip on her throat one finger at a time, "I've been imagining bending you over this fucking table since you walked in the front door."

"Yes." She complies as she hops down and drapes her top half over the table.

"Good girl," I praise before I smack her ass hard, making her let out a sharp yelp. I bend forward, wrapping my hand around her throat again, growling in her ear. "After this. You are mine. There will be no one else. Understood?"

"Yes, Daddy," she moans as she backs her ass against my groin. Her perfectly round tight ass grinding against me has me groaning in need. I yank the button open to my jeans, lowering the zipper, and smack her ass once more before shucking down my pants and briefs. Releasing my throbbing dick is a welcome relief knowing I'm going to feel her wrapped around it.

I glide my crown along the slit of her pussy, tapping her clit with my cock. "You're so wet for me, Kitten." I groan, slapping her ass again.

"I'm always wet when I'm around you," she mewls.

Fuck me.

I slide the tip of my cock inside her tight entrance. The gasp that leaves her mouth at my thickness has me smirking. "I'll take it slow, Ry. Don't worry." I soothe as I enter another inch.

"Fuck, Grey." She whimpers so beautifully.

"Remember, we don't want them to hear us, Kitten."

I smack her ass again as I pull out a little, just to slide back in further. She's so fucking tight. When I'm finally fully seated inside her I give her a moment to adjust.

"Are you ok?" I ask before I start really moving.

"Yes," she breathes.

With the confirmation I need, I pull out to just the crown before thrusting back inside her. She whimpers again each time my balls slap against her clit.

"You're doing so well, taking me so deep, beautiful," I praise as I wrap my arm around her waist, my fingers finding her swollen clit, pressing firmly as I continue fucking her.

"As much as I want this to last, I've been imagining this for so long." I grunt as I thrust into her again.

"I need you to come with me. Then I will worship your body all fucking night, I will have you trembling with orgasm after orgasm," I whisper in her ear.

"Fuck yes," she cries out softly, as the walls of her pussy ripple around my cock. I pump into her once more before finding my release, exploding inside her. I run my hand down her spine before allowing her to stand back up. Tucking myself back into my pants, she dresses and stares up at me. I crowd her space, wrapping my arm around her waist and cupping the nape of her neck, lowering my lips to hers for a quick kiss.

"You took me so well." I praise her again. She just smiles up at me with a content look on her face. "Tell me you don't have to take them home." I whisper into her ear.

"No, Hadley drove us." She raises her brow at me in question.

"Good, let's say goodbye so I can take you home and worship you the way you deserve."

Chapter Thirteen

T he girls give a knowing look as soon as they see us walk out of the room together. I tell them that Grey offered to drive me home so they didn't have to double back, letting Hadley get home to show Connor her tattoo sooner, like we all knew she was dying to do.

Hadley wraps her arms around me and whispers into my ear, "We're going to need all the details tomorrow."

She presses a kiss to my cheek before grabbing Pickle's hand and walking out. As soon as they're out of sight, Grey grabs me around the waist, pulling me into his arms and pressing a kiss against my mouth. I melt into him as his tongue parts my lips. It's over too fast and he pulls away from me.

"Let's get out of here before I fuck you again in the lobby," he growls.

I unlock my front door, barely getting inside the threshold before Grey slams the door behind us and I'm being pressed face first against the wall. He has a grip on my wrists holding them above my head as he grinds into my ass. "I don't think you know just how long I've wanted you, Ry," Grey growls with a soft whisper in my ear, his warm breath bathing my skin as he snakes an arm around my waist, slowly trailing down my stomach until he reaches the waistband of my pants. His thumb hooks underneath, dragging it down on one side before sliding to the other, pulling them down to expose my blue boy shorts. He groans appreciatively at the sight of my ass.

"Did you wear these for me today?"

"Yes," I giggle.

He releases my hands, allowing my arms to drop to my sides as he pulls my pants down to my feet. He helps me step out of them before lifting me in his arms and carrying me to my couch. He sets me down and pulls his shirt off over his head. I gasp at the vision before me. His entire torso and chest are covered in intricate lines and designs, and I spot the beautiful lily on his chest, remembering it from when we were younger. But we're not those young kids anymore. He's grown so much.

Muscles line his body that I didn't know existed in real life before seeing this man. The v at his hips has my imagination running wild even though I've already felt just how big he is.

"Grey" I whisper, staring at him, our eyes lock and without a word he closes the distance between us once more.

His hands tangle in my hair and our lips crash together again. He fucks my mouth with his tongue, leaving me panting with need when we come up for air. I manage to roll us over so he's sitting on the couch beneath me, my legs straddling his thick thighs. I press light kisses against his neck, moving down to his chest. I nip and suck at the beautiful artwork displayed across his body. He groans when I slide down between his legs.

"I've waited long enough to taste you, don't you think?"

I smirk up at him as I run my hands down his defined abs to the fly of his pants, unhooking the button of his jeans and lowering the zipper to free him. He's hard as stone. The silky smooth skin feels glorious in my hand. A bead of precum pools at the tip, and I lower my head, swirling my tongue around the crown to get every bit of him I can. We both moan in pleasure as I hollow my cheeks and take him into my mouth.

"Fuck, Ry. Your mouth is sinful." He groans as his hands tangle in my hair.

I moan around his cock at his praise.

"Yea, Kitten. You like making me feel good?" he breathes.

"Mmm" is all I manage as I suck him deeper into my throat. I grip his hips as I force him further into my mouth, swallowing him down. He's so thick that my jaw is already sore, but the heat pooling in my core at his pleasure has me willing to continue. I release him to the tip, gently grazing my teeth over the sensitive skin before sucking him back into my mouth. His control snaps when he feels the back of my throat again.

"Fuck, baby girl," he groans as he grips my head, holding me in place as he fucks my face.

"Your mouth feels so goddamn good."

Tears begin running down my cheeks and a sense of pride takes hold as I dig my nails into his hips, sucking his length every time he thrusts into my mouth.

"I'm gonna fill your pretty little mouth and I wanna see you swallow it all." He issues the command and I moan in response.

I cup his balls, tugging gently on the next thrust and a string of curses falls from his lips as he explodes into my mouth. The hot stream of his release tastes so good, his salty flavor giving me a high I didn't know I'd enjoy. Before I can swallow, he releases me to see my face. Being the good girl that I am, I do as Daddy commands and open my mouth wide, showing him my mouth filled with his release, before sealing my lips and swallowing. The taste of him in the back of my throat quickly becomes my new favorite flavor.

"Jesus christ, Ry," he groans as he pulls me back onto his lap, pressing his lips against mine again.

"Mine" he repeats his declaration from earlier, planting a soft kiss against my throat.

"Yours," I whisper in response.

Chapter Fourteen

My eyes flutter open at the sunlight peeking through the curtains. I groan and attempt to roll over when I realize Ryan is lying on my bare chest, sound asleep.

It wasn't a dream.

I spent the rest of the night worshiping her perfect body, as promised. We didn't fall asleep until the early hours of dawn. The memories come rushing back to me. The way her pussy feels around my cock is better than any fantasy I could ever dream up. She is so responsive when I touch her. My dick stiffens at the memories.

I snake my arms around Ry as I roll over on top of her, settling my hips between her thighs. I press my lips to her forehead and trail down her face to her neck, sucking and nipping at the sensitive flesh behind her ear. She stirs under me, softly moaning and grinding against my length.

"Morning, Kitten." My voice is gravelly from sleep.

"Morning," she murmurs and hooks her legs around my waist. "I like waking up like this." She smiles as her eyes slowly blink open.

"Me too, gorgeous." I press another soft kiss against her lips. "I need to get up though, and if you continue grinding against me, I'm going to have to explain to your brother that I blew him off so I could continue nailing you to the bed. As much as I'd love for that to be the case, he only has today to help me with a few big things at Dad's house."

She stiffens under me at the mention of Jack.

"Oh," she says quietly and loosens her hold.

I grip her chin, tilting her face to meet my gaze so she's got nowhere to look but in my eyes.

"Kitten, I'm not hiding you. I will tell him as soon as I see him. I just need the manpower in getting some big shit out of the house." I press a soft kiss against her lips, putting a little more pressure around her throat. "I told you last night. You're mine."

"Ok." She smiles up at me.

"I also need to check on Ellie. She's not a fan of being left alone overnight and I doubt Jack let her sleep with him," I say as I stand up.

"Excuse me, who is Ellie?" Her voice comes out as a shrill gasp.

"What do you mean?" I smirk at her.

"Grey, I'm not going to be a side piece. Who the fuck is Ellie?" The panic in her voice is adorable.

"My cat." I fail to hold in my laugh.

I walk into Jack's house to find him sitting on the couch, his head resting on the back cushion with a very large man's face buried between his legs. We never talked about it, but I always suspected he was attracted to men. His eyes flicker open as I walk past, heading towards the guest room where I've been sleeping. Jack's face pales when he sees me. I just smile and cheer. "Get it, man!"

Entering my room, I find Ellie asleep on the bed. "Hi, pretty girl." I sit next to her on the bed, petting her for several moments before getting up and filling her food and water bowls. "I'm sorry I didn't come home, but you already know there's only one girl I would stay out all night for." I smile to myself as the memories invade my thoughts again. I make my way into the ensuite bathroom and turn on the shower before peeling off my clothes. Stepping into the hot stream, I lean with my hands against the wall, enjoying the wet heat cascading down my tight muscles.

I can't believe she's finally mine.

I feel a smile tugging at the corner of my lips as I reluctantly wash her scent off of me. When I finally emerge from my shower, a towel tied around my waist, I walk into my room to find Jack sitting on the bed with Ellie.

"So," his voice shakes. "Are we good?"

"Why wouldn't we be?" I raise a brow at him as I grab a pair of boxer briefs from the dresser, pulling them on under my towel.

"Well, with Bennett?" He looks at me like I've lost my mind.

"Did you not finish or something? I can't help ya there, but I'm not gonna stop you if you want to hang around here a bit longer to have some more fun with him. I'll get some coffee." I smirk at him while I pull a shirt from the dresser and over my head before grabbing a pair of jeans from the bottom drawer.

"I - uh." Jack stumbles over his words before he continues. "Yea if you wanna give me an hour or two I can meet you at the house?"

"Sure, man. Have fun." I pull my socks and shoes on before walking out past him with my phone in hand. "Just call me if you need longer," I yell back over my shoulder.

I unlock my phone and send a message to Ryan who responds quickly.

[Text Message]

Grey

Kitten, are you still home?

Ryan

No, I just left. Everything ok?

Grey

Yeah, just a delay in the start of my day and I miss you already. I wanted to see you again.

Ryan

I'm meeting the girls at Mud House. If you don't mind the questions you're going to get, you're welcome to join us. I miss you too.

Oh, this is going to be fun. Hadley has been trying to get us together for years. She's going to have a fucking field day once she finds out.

I walk into Mud House to find Hadley and Kat standing at the counter ordering. Looking around, I spot Ryan at a table with her laptop open, unaware of her surroundings. I see Hadley look over at me and smile from my peripheral. She waves me over, but I promptly ignore the signal and march over to Ryan, who is still oblivious to my presence. I push the screen of her laptop down and pull her into my arms. She gasps as my mouth finds hers. My tongue parts her lips and our kiss becomes heated, the taste of her peppermint mocha coffee fresh in her mouth. The lust from last night hasn't gone anywhere; hell, if anything, I want this woman more than I did before. Ryan melts into me, her body conforming to mine as she wraps her arms around my neck, holding me in place. It may be minutes or hours before we finally pull apart to find Hadley and Kat standing in front of us.

"Holy shit!" Hadley squeals. "It's about fucking time!" She pulls us both into a tight embrace, Kat's mouth still agape as we all take our seats around the table.

"Thanks, Hadley. That's not embarrassing at all." Ryan flinches as she nestles in tighter to my hold.

"Y'all totally fucked at the tattoo shop last night didn't you?" Kat finally finds her voice.

"Oh, my god, you did!" Hadley shrieks. Ryan doesn't respond, waiting for me to take the lead. Before I can respond, I hear a text notification and pull my phone from my pocket.

Jack

Leaving here in fifteen minutes.

"You can tell them whatever you want. Jack just finished what he was doing so I have to get to the house. I just wanted to see you again." I smile as I press a soft kiss against her lips. "I'll pick you up for dinner at seven tonight." I wink at her before waving to the other two and walking back out to my car.

Chapter Fifteen

"What the hell happened? You swore up and down he'd never, and now he marches in here determined to make certain anyone present knows you're his." Pickle's question pulls me from the spell the kisses had me under.

"Yea, it was hot as hell." Hadley giggles

I smile to myself before responding. "He's been like that since last night, told me that as soon as we took it all the way, I was his." I smirk, my face heating at the memory.

"Oh, hell, I love when Connor does that." Hadley giggles as she stands from her seat and pulls me into a hug. "I know I said this before but it's so about time!"

"As long as he treats you well, babe." Is the only thing Pickle says. She's been uncharacteristically quiet lately.

"How is everything with you and Clay?" Hadley asks, noticing the tension.

"Oh, we're great," Pickle smiles brightly before she changes the subject. We continue chatting for a few hours before Pickle and Hadley have a session at the gym to get to.

I stay at Mud House for a while longer, working on edits from last night and interacting on social media. The comments have been sparse lately, but I'm hoping different kinds of content will bring in new followers. Once the edits of Hadley and Grey's tattoo session are complete, I post the pictures to my Instagram showcasing the process tagging them both.

The caption reads:

@RySnaps *My best friend, taking the next steps in her healing journey. So much love and care put into these incredible pieces of art. #survivor*

Grey comments first.

@GreysInk *It was an honor helping my Hellion heal. You got some amazing shots, Kitten.*

@HadleysLife *I'm so happy with your work, butt-face! Connor wants you to work on one for him too!*

@HadleysLife *Get a room you two.*

@GreysInk *We will in a few hours, don't worry, Hellion.*

Oh, my god. I close the app, unsure how to even respond to the two of them. I look up to see Kayleigh smiling at me with a knowing look in her eyes as she serves customers at the counter. I pack up my laptop and wave goodbye before I head out to my Jeep.

Hadley and Pickle are on a video chat with me as I change into yet another outfit for tonight. Grey gave me no hints as to where we're going so I have no clue what to wear. I pull out a deep blue mini dress with a plunging neckline that dips nearly to my navel. The hem just covers my ass but the look on their faces tells me this is the one.

"Babe, that is the hottest thing I've ever seen on a woman." Pickle's eyes are bright as she praises my choice.

"Yea, you are so getting lucky tonight if you wear that." Hadley chuckles.

"Hopefully it will work for wherever he's taking me. I don't know if Jack knows yet. He hasn't called me or anything so I don't know if we're going anywhere in town." I know Grey said he'd tell Jack but since I haven't received any contact from my overprotective brother, I don't know if he has.

It's six forty-five when I hear a knock on my front door. I say goodbye to the girls before ending the call. I unlock the door and pull it open, giddy for whatever Grey has planned. My smile falters when I see Jack in the doorway looking more anxious than a drug dealer with a brick of coke in their car.

"What's wrong?" I gasp as I move aside to let him in.

"Grey knows," he blurts out as he paces back and forth. "He says he's ok with it but I don't know how to act around him now."

"Wait, he knows what?" I ask as I take a seat on the couch, crossing my legs..

"About Bennet," Jack groans as he collapses next to me on the couch.

"Wait, I thought everyone knew about Benny?" I raise a brow at my brother.

"Everyone *here* does. You know I don't use social media." He groans, "Grey and I haven't talked about relationships since before he left because of how much we all hated Raven!"

I stare at him, "Grey is the last person to judge you. He loves you, and as long as you're happy he's going to love Benny just like I do." I wrap an arm around Jack's shoulders.

"I know you're right. How the hell do I formally introduce them though? He walked in on us!" he shouts as he looks at me. His eyebrows scrunch together as he takes in my outfit. "Wait, what are you wearing? Where the hell are you going in that?"

Grey of course chooses that moment to just walk through my front door. "Hey, Kitten." His face falls when he sees Jack. "Everything ok, bud?"

Jack's gaze swings quickly between me and Grey, and I can see the wheels turning in his head as he pieces together the scene before him. "You tell me, Greyson. What the fuck are you doing here when my sister is dressed in that?" He throws his thumb over his shoulder pointing at me. I stand to get between the two of them.

"We're going out for dinner," I say confidently.

Grey walks to me and wraps an arm around my waist protectively, pulling me to his side and whispering into my hair, "Give us a minute, gorgeous." I step aside as Grey speaks to my brother. "I had planned on telling you this morning, but it slipped my mind when I got back to your place." He raises a brow at him.

"Oh, the fuck it did. I don't care if you walked in on me nailing Bennett over the kitchen table!" He snarls at Grey, "You had all fucking day to talk to me about it, too, you asshole! She's my sister!"

"I know, I should have found the time today. I'm sorry." He takes a step further from me and my heart drops. "I'm not going to apologize for wanting to be with Ryan though. I've had feelings for her for years, which is partially why I left, Jack. I was worried about ruining our friendship because of how you are with her." His declaration has tears welling in my eyes.

Jack moves so quickly I don't realize what's happening until he has Grey tackled onto the floor, pummeling his face with his fists. I scream out for them to stop but it's like neither of them can hear me. Grey somehow ends up flipping the two of them so he's above Jack, pinning his hands down at his sides.

"Take a breath, man. I may have deserved one punch but I'm not going to allow you to hit me again." He snarls, "Are you good?" Jack nods and Grey stands over him, helping him up.

Grey walks over to me, his face bloody from the blows. "Are you ok, Kitten?" I nod as he glides his fingers down my cheek before I move around Grey to check on Jack who knocks me out of the way to get to Grey. I land roughly on the couch, stunned by my brother's actions. It takes a moment to register Grey is on top of Jack again, but this time he's hitting him over and over again.

"Grey! Stop!" I shriek out a sob. "Please! I'm ok!" Grey's darkened eyes meet mine before he leaps off of Jack, coming to check on me again.

"If you ever touch her like that again, I will fucking kill you, family or not. You will not hurt her," he growls as he pulls me into his arms, shielding me from Jack.

"Are you ok, sis?" Jack asks in a gruff voice, wiping the blood from his already swelling nose.

"I'm fine. Go home. I'll talk to you tomorrow." I don't look at him, too upset by his outburst to meet his eye.

Jack walks out, closing my front door behind him.

"We're going to talk about you not locking your door, Kitten." Grey pulls away from me just enough to raise my chin to meet his gaze. "But first, I've been wanting to do this since I left the coffee shop." He lowers his head, pressing his lips to mine. His hands snake up my back until both are gripping fistfuls of my hair holding my head in place as he keeps control of the kiss. His tongue swipes against my lips, and my mouth instinctively parts, opening for him. His tongue clashes against mine, tangling with each other. I raise my hands to his neck and jump up, wrapping my legs around his waist. His moans fill my mouth when my hot center grinds against his hard length. We part, both panting for breath. After that kiss, there's no way we're going anywhere for dinner.

"As much as I want you, I need to get you cleaned up." I smile, pressing another chaste kiss against his lips before sliding down his body. He grabs my ass, groaning into my hair when I'm back on the floor. I grab his hand and pull him into the bathroom with me. I notice his quick glance at my shower, but my suction cup dildo is away this time, thankfully.

"Sit." I instruct, pointing to the toilet.

I grab a washcloth from the linen closet and run warm water to dampen it enough to clean the blood from his face.

"I'll accept you being in control right now, but as soon as my face is healed, I'm going to show you exactly why you like me having control." He smirks.

His eyes are already pretty swollen, and I know tomorrow it's going to be even worse. Yet he's still the most beautiful man I've ever seen.

"Yes, Daddy," I giggle before my tone becomes serious again. "But this may hurt. Are you ready?"

"Do your worst," Grey looks up at me, his expression unreadable.

Chapter Sixteen

We finally make it to Ryan's room and she's lying back, propped up on her elbows and staring up at me. My adrenaline has been racing since the fight, and as much as I need to taste her again, my eyes are busted up too badly to have her riding my face the way I want. The thought of the pressure of her thighs squeezing my head as she comes makes my dick twitch, but my face can't handle it right now. Not that it stops me from burying it between her legs, inhaling the sweet scent. I raise the tiny excuse of a dress up over her hips to reveal she's bare. I look up at her and I raise my brow, or at least I try to. It's unclear what my face actually does because of the swelling.

"You were going to go out like this?"

"Well, panties don't really work with this dress." She shrugs her shoulders, a wicked grin plastered across her face.

"Oh Kitten, I think the only thing that works with this dress is if I'm fucking you in it or it's on the floor." I hover over her, pressing a soft kiss against her lips before hooking my arms around her legs and pulling her to the edge of the bed. She's spread open for me, watching and waiting. I pull my henley over my head, tossing it onto the chair by her bed, followed quickly by my jeans and boxer briefs.

I close the little bit of distance between us and tap the crown of my cock against her clit. She cries out at the pressure.

"Grey, please. I've been thinking about you all day."

"I know, Kitten. I haven't stopped thinking about you either."

I grip my dick, my hand wrapped firmly around the base, letting out a groan. I feel it throbbing in my hand as she wriggles beneath me.

"Patience," I scold.

I glide the tip along her lips, feeling the proof of her arousal drenching me already, and I haven't even gotten started. I lean down, hovering over her again, pressing my lips to hers before wrapping an arm around her waist and flipping us over so that she's on top of me. Her legs straddle my hips as she squeaks in surprise at the shift in position.

"Take what you need, beautiful." I smirk up at her.

She presses a soft kiss against my lips again before sitting up and guiding my cock into her entrance. We both groan as my length disappears inside her.

"Fuck me, your pussy is perfect."

Ryan's giggle is mixed with a moan when I thrust upwards, fully seating myself inside her. She starts to slowly bounce on my stiffness, her hips undulating each time she reaches the base. I grip her hips, raising the little dress higher up her hips, exposing more of her impeccable body. I sit up while she's bouncing on my cock and pull the dress up over her head tossing it to the side revealing her beautiful, perky tits.

"Jesus christ, Ry. You're amazing," I groan into her neck, pressing a light kiss against the sensitive spot that drove her wild last night.

She cries out and speeds up her movements. I slide my hands up her body, feeling her smooth, warm skin under my hands leaving goose-bumps in their wake. I reach her breasts, cupping one in my hand gently, massaging the sensitive tissue. I lower my head to her chest pulling her nipple into my mouth, grazing my teeth against the hard peak. Ryan's moans fill the room as I bite down a little harder.

My girl likes pain.

I smile to myself and smack her ass hard before removing my mouth from her.

"Oh god, you feel so good," she moans, her head thrown back as she continues fucking herself with my dick.

"God's a little formal, Kitten." I grin up at her before gripping her hips and holding her still so I can thrust deep inside her. "You take my cock so well."

"Oh. Fuck. Me," she sobs as she throws her head back. Her breasts bounce in my face with each thrust. I roll us back over to find a better position angling myself just right to hit the most sensitive spot inside her. "Grey, Grey, Grey!" she chants my name as I continue fucking her.

"Your pussy feels so good, I can feel you tightening around me baby girl."

Thrust.

"You."

Thrust.

"Were."

Thrust.

"Made for me."

My balls tighten as I feel her detonate around my cock, her walls convulsing as she comes apart. My orgasm follows quickly as I empty inside her, filling her with my seed.

I collapse on top of her, pressing soft kisses to her neck and chest before finding her lips again.

A loud knock jolts me awake. I open my eyes to find Ryan still asleep on my chest. I smile before pressing a soft kiss against her hair and slipping out from under her. I pull on my underwear and walk out to the front door. Opening it, I find Jack standing there with all my belongings, including Ellie, in tow.

"What the fuck, Jack? You're really going to be this much of an ass about me and your sister?" I growl as I take Ellie's carrier from him, stepping out of the way so he can come in. I pull Ellie out of the crate and take a seat on the couch, "Are you ok, sweet girl?" I ask as I cuddle her close.

"You are ridiculous with that cat. You realize that, right?" Jack asks as he puts my stuff down in the living room. His hands are on his hips as he looks around the apartment. "Where is she?"

"Sleeping." I respond quietly.

"It's fucked up that you pulled this now when you know you're only here for what, a week? Maybe two?" He continues, "She's going to get hurt and I'm going to have to kill you." He growls.

"I have no intentions of hurting her." I sigh as I run my hand down Ellie's back. She's already curled on my lap, purring. "We haven't talked out the fine details yet, but this isn't a fling, Jack. Not to me."

He rolls his eyes. "I'll believe that when I see it. I'm not fucking around, motherfucker. I will end you." He turns on his heel and walks out the door.

I hear the bedroom door open before Ryan steps out in my Henley and no pants. *Oh christ, my dick is awake now.* Thank fuck she waited until Jack was gone.

"Good morning." She smiles as she walks towards us, rubbing the sleep from her eyes. She comes to a stop with a sharp gasp. "Who is this beauty?" She drops to her knees in front of me as she pets and cuddles Ellie.

Oh yea, I'm fucked.

"Morning beautiful, you on your knees like this is a great way to start the day." I wink at her.

"Sorry, there's a furry animal here, you lost your priority status." She giggles as she climbs up and sits next to me, snuggling into my side. "So I take it Jack came by?"

"Yea. He's not ready to talk shit out yet." I sigh into her hair. "I'll take my stuff to my dad's and stay there for now," I murmur as I absentmind-edly pet Ellie.

"Or," she pauses. "You could stay here. It'll be much more entertain-ing for me, and bonus, I won't be going through as many batteries." She looks up at me through her dark lashes, a wicked grin on her beautiful face.

"Oh, Kitten, you won't be going through any batteries as long as I'm around," I smirk at her lifting Ellie off my lap and placing her onto the floor before pushing Ryan down on the couch and hovering over her, my lips crashing against hers.

Chapter Seventeen

I'm so deliciously sore from the last two days. Grey has had me using muscles I forgot I had. I pull my camera bag over my shoulder as I climb out of my Jeep, noticing a woman standing by the door of my studio. She's beautiful, with long dark wavy hair cascading down her shoulders. Her eyes are covered by large sunglasses, and her button nose and full red lips have me mentally fanning myself.

"Hi! I'm Ryan, may I help you?" I ask as I walk towards her.

"Oh, hi! I'm Luna. I'm your one o'clock session. I just got here a little early and since it's so nice I didn't want to wait in my car. "

I glance at my watch seeing it's only noon but shrug. The sooner I can get the session done the sooner I can talk to Pickle and Hadley.

"Come on in. Give me about twenty minutes to set everything up and we can get started early." I smile at her as I unlock my studio. Opening the door, I allow her to walk in before following.

Damn, she has a tight ass too.

I spend the next twenty minutes getting my equipment set up, making sure that the lighting is set to the correct direction and intensity before we begin. I remember her form said she was interested in a partial nude boudoir session. I meander to the thermostat, lowering the temp in the room before stepping back out to the lobby.

"Let me show you to the room where you can get changed." I smile at her before turning towards the back of the studio.

"So what made you decide to do the shoot?" I ask.

As we enter the changing room, she sets her bag on the oversized burnt orange couch. Table lamps brighten up the space from opposite corners.

"I went through a rough breakup. Really, I've been wanting to do this for me for a while," she says shyly.

"Then let's do this for you, gorgeous." I wink at her before continuing. "You can leave your bags in here, and then if you have a second outfit you want to change into you can come back here when we get done with the first one."

I step back into the hall and walk back to the front of the studio, grabbing my phone from my bag to find a text message.

A photo of him laying shirtless on my couch with Ellie lying on his stomach is attached.

I shake my head with a goofy ass grin on my face. This man is going to be the death of me.

As I'm bending down to put my phone back in my bag, I get a notification from Instagram, a comment on the photos I took of Hadley's tattoo

@IngridsPerfection *Your art is almost as beautiful as you.*

I roll my eyes at the obvious flirtation aimed towards Grey just as Luna walks out of the room. I offer a bright smile before I bend down and place my phone back in my bag. I stand to see her right in front of me in a silky black robe.

"Oh, hi," I giggle nervously at her closeness, the scent of her strawberry lotion is so strong I have to take a step back. Her sunglasses are off now and her eyes are the most beautiful shade of silver I've ever seen.

"Let's go in here and we can get started." I wave my hand in the direction of the room before moving around her to walk toward the closed door. Once inside, she removes her silk robe to expose a set of red lingerie that would make a Victoria's Secret Angel jealous, the sheer lace leaving nothing to the imagination. Her nipples are already pebbling through the thin cups of her bra. Her breasts are so full they're nearly popping out as it is. There is a red choker, or maybe, is that a collar? I swallow hard. Her ass looks even better than I imagined in the boyshorts.

"Where would you like me?" She smiles sweetly at me.

"Let's start on the bench here." I point before instructing her on the first pose to try out with the vibe she was going for. We move seamlessly around the space as I give her instructions on body placement. She's a fantastic model; she looks flawless and she's so easy to work with. We go over the allotted time for a session but, because she was early, it won't affect my plans.

"Oh, this was such an amazing experience, Ryan. Thank you so much!" Luna squeals as she stands from the bed, her white heels clicking on the floor as she rushes over, wrapping me in a hug. I freeze, unsure what to do since she's only in a black thong. I pat her back softly, offering a gentle smile as I step away and out of her embrace.

"You are most welcome, gorgeous. I can have these done tomorrow evening. Would you like me to post them on my instagram after you review them?"

"Oh you can post them anywhere! I'm sure they're going to be wonderful! Thank you so much!" she squeals as she skips back to the changing room. I chuckle to myself as I remove the memory card from my camera and slide it into my laptop. I sit at the desk in the lobby as I scroll through her shots. I got so many good angles, she is extremely photogenic. Her eyes shine in every single picture. It's incredible.

After I park my car at our favorite dive bar, Finley's, I step out and spot both of the girls' cars in the lot before I walk toward the entrance. I open the door to see Hadley and Pickle sitting at a table with drinks already waiting. I walk quickly toward them, wrapping my arms around Pickle and pressing a kiss to her cheek, before moving to Hadley and pulling her in for a tight hug.

"Spill it, woman." Pickle giggles as she lifts her glass to her lips, taking a sip.

"Well, we never made it out of the house last night." I pause, taking a drink of my cocktail. "First, Jack showed up freaking out because Grey walked in on him and Benny. Apparently Grey didn't know they're a thing."

"Wait, how did he not know?" Hadley raises her brow.

"Jack isn't on social media and he's never talked about his love life with Grey," I explain. "Then Grey walked into my place when Jack was there and when Jack realized I had on the skimpiest dress I own, he put two and two together."

My words are cut off by a notification from my phone. I pull it out, holding it in my lap as I continue.

"Jack attacked Grey and then we thought he was done but when Grey was checking on me Jack accidentally pushed me trying to get back at Grey so he went after Jack." The words rush out of my mouth.

"It was a shit show. Now Grey and Ellie are staying with me." I smirk.

"Who the fuck is Ellie?" Pickle asks, a tinge of jealousy in her voice.

"His cat, did you not follow his instagram at the tattoo shop?" Hadley raises a brow.

"I may have followed it but I didn't stalk it." Pickle rolls her eyes.

I laugh as I pull my phone out of my lap and check the notifications.

Grey

> *Don't show Hellion.*

Attached is a picture of a pec covered in fresh ink, a claddagh symbol with baby dandelions weaving around it displayed in a beautiful design with such intricate details. It's breathtaking.

Ryan

> *Oh my god, she's going to die! It's amazing!*

I don't bother hiding the smile when I look back up at the girls. Pickle makes a gagging noise like she's over me already. Hadley's smile mirrors my own. Oh, if only she knew.

Chapter Eighteen

I get back to Ryan's a little before ten at night. She's still at Finley's with Kat and Hadley when I arrive, the windows dark. I walk up to the front door to find a note attached, written in nearly illegible handwriting, with a picture of Ryan and I from Nat's shop stapled to it.

Soon.

What the hell? I grab my phone out of my pocket and dial quickly, surprised when he answers on the second ring.

"What's wrong?" Jack's panicked voice comes through the phone.

"There's a creepy ass note and a picture of us on Ryan's door. She's not home yet," I explain.

"I'm around the corner at Bennett's. I'll be there in five minutes." He hangs up before I can go into any more detail.

I unlock the door and slowly open it, flipping the light switch as soon as my hand can fit between the crack of the open door and the wall. When the room is illuminated, I push the door open further before stepping inside, looking around.

Nothing looks out of place. Before I take another step I feel a hand grip my shoulder. I turn around, my fist ready to connect with whoever is there. Jack blocks my punch and takes a step back shaking his head.

"You're a fucking idiot walking in here by yourself." He shakes his head and lets out a sigh.

"Sorry man." I pat his shoulder. "Thank you for coming."

"She's my sister, and you may be a fucking idiot, but you're family too." He rolls his eyes before motioning for me to continue into the house.

We slowly walk through the house, checking each room. We find Ellie sound asleep on Ryan's bed purring up a storm, and I let out a long breath when I see she's ok. Jack and I walk out to the living room and sit on the couch.

"Let me see it." Jack holds out his hand.

I hand it over, thanking whatever guardian angel is looking out for me that it's just a picture of us kissing in the lobby and not when I had her bent over the table in the back room after her tattoo was done.

"This is through his front window. Someone was watching from outside," he says as he holds the picture closer to his face. "Did you notice anyone before you left?"

"Uh, no. We were a bit distracted." I admit

"As much as I'm not happy about you and Ryan, you're adults and if we're honest, it's been a long time coming." He pauses, scrubbing a hand down his face in frustration. "I swear to all that is holy. If I have to kill you, I'm gonna be pissed." Jack groans as he sits on the couch next to me. "I brought your shit over here because I already know you're going to be staying with Ryan the rest of the time you're here anyway. And, I like your cat and all, but not the howling at night because she misses you."

I hear a car door close and feet padding up the walk just a moment before the door knob twists and Ryan walks in and freezes in the doorway, looking between Jack and I.

"Did you boys kiss and make up?" Her smile is infectious.

"Yes, shithead," Jack answers for me. I elbow him in the ribs.

"Just because we're cool doesn't mean I want you talking to her like that." I laugh as he punches my shoulder.

Ryan walks over and sits on my lap, pressing a soft kiss against my lips. "Hi."

"Hi, beautiful." I smile at her, staring into her beautiful chocolate eyes.

"Ew, I'm right here. You realize that, right?" Jack groans.

"Why yes, big brother, I do." she smiles brightly at him before scooting off of my lap and onto the couch, "So, what did I miss?"

Jack and I share a look before he nods. I explain what I came back here to find and why I called Jack, showing her the note and picture.

"I've gotten random notes like this at the studio, but never here," she admits, shrugging her shoulders like it's no big deal.

"You what?!" Jack screams. "Have you contacted the police? Does Bennett know?" He rapid fires the questions at her.

"I filed a report with someone at the station, but I don't know if they told Benny. They said they can't do anything because they haven't hurt me." She rolls her eyes.

I feel my heart rate increasing, and my vision blurs as every dark and depraved scenario runs through my mind. I stand up and start pacing back and forth across her carpeted living room.

"Grey," I hear Ryan's voice whisper through the rage fueled haze. "You're going all Tarzan on me, baby. I'm ok"

I turn to see her standing, slowly approaching me like a wild animal she's afraid to spook. I march over, gripping the back of her neck and pulling her waist against me.

"I will find out who the fuck is behind this and I will end them." I growl before pressing a rough kiss against her lips.

Jack must have called Bennett without me noticing while Ry was calming me down because twenty minutes later there's a loud knock on the door. Jack stands from where he sat on the couch to answer it. He opens the door to a very large, familiar looking man with a broad chest. His inky colored hair is cropped short, and he's wearing a holster over his shoulders with a Glock on either side of his chest.

"Hey King," the newcomer says to Jack as they greet each other with a passionate kiss.

Oh, that's why he looks familiar.

"Grey, Bennett, Bennett, Grey," Jack formally introduces us. "He's a detective with the Central Falls PD." Jack beams, obnoxiously proud of his man.

"Nice to meet you, Bennett." I reach out to shake his hand. He takes mine in a firm grip in greeting.

"Benny," Ryan's voice is full of warmth as she stands, taking a few steps to meet his large form before wrapping herself around him.

My jaw clenches at the affection between the two. I know it's a brotherly hug but another man touching her has my blood boiling. They separate after a moment and she returns to my side. We all sit along the large sectional and explain what happened, once again.

Chapter Nineteen

It's been a week since I told Grey and Jack about the random notes I found at my studio and Jack tried insisting either he or Grey stay with me while I'm working. Since most of my clients have been doing boudoir shoots, that didn't seem like a viable option. These women won't feel comfortable with a man hanging around. Besides, statistics show that it's highly unlikely a woman would be behind this.

Grey dropped me off this morning, insisting that he take me to and pick me up from work. I could say I hate it but really, it makes me feel warm and fuzzy that he's being so protective. It's different now than it was when I was a kid. Back then, he and Jack would gang up on anyone who showed any interest in me. However, it was always very brotherly between the two of them.

It's just after ten, and I'm finally finished with the edits from Luna's shoot. Annoyed with myself that it's taken longer than usual to get the edits done with everything that's happened this week, I send off the final edits and wait for a response before I post them.

I scroll through my Instagram account seeing several new comments on old posts.

@IngridsPerfection Love the way you capture your own beauty in every photo.

@IngridsPerfection She's not as pretty as you.

@IngridsPerfection You take my breath away.

Before I can look any further into the posts, the front door to my studio opens, I close the app and put my phone back on the desk. A tiny blonde woman, shorter than Hadley, walks in. A bright smile spreads across her face when she sees me.

"Hi! I'm Mandi!" She beams.

"Hi Mandi, I'm Ryan. It's so nice to meet you." I smile back at her. "Are you my ten-thirty?"

I've been looking forward to this girls' night all day. Hadley, Pickle and I are all snuggled up on the couch together rewatching The Office, and we're currently on the episode where Jim and Pam kiss for the first time. Hadley and I cheer when Jim walks back into the reception area of the Dunder Mifflin office and pulls her into a kiss without saying another word, both of us acting like we've never seen it before.

"Pickle," I poke Kat's shoulder. "You ok? You've been oddly quiet tonight. You love this episode."

"I'm just tired. I've been getting pretty intense workouts lately." A wicked smile crosses her face.

"Oh, you are so getting nailed!" I shriek and stop the next episode from starting.

"It's not like we hadn't been having sex before, it's just different now. It's more intense," she admits. " My vagina has never been so happy to have a night off," she giggles.

"Just how much sex are you having?" Hadley chimes in from the other side of me.

"Uhm, well. A few times a day," she admits.

"Do I need to step up my game?" Grey suddenly appears in the hallway to my bedroom, his muscular, ink covered chest on full display. The three of us scream, Hadley throws one of the pillows from the couch in his direction which hits him square in the face. She and Pickle cheer at the connection.

"Fuck. Me," I pant. "You scared the shit out of me." I stand up, walk over to him, and tangle my hands in his hair. I raise on my tip toes and press my lips against his for a quick kiss. "I'm quite satisfied, thank you." I smile up at him. He grips my ass lifting me into his arms, my legs latching around his waist as I squeal in surprise. He raises a hand to my face, caressing my cheek with his fingers before taking my chin between his thumb and forefinger, pulling my face back to his, kissing me like no one is around. I melt into him, quietly moaning into his mouth.

After maybe a minute I hear a throat clear behind me and pull away, my face red. It's usually Hadley that acts like this with Connor. I can't even remember the last time I forgot my surroundings from a damn kiss. *And what a fucking kiss it was.* I groan and slide down the length of Grey's body, feeling his hard bulge as I do.

"We're gonna go then." Hadley smirks at Grey and I. She and Pickle are both standing by the couch picking up their bags. Hadley reaches me first, snaking her arms around my waist for a hug. "I'm so fucking happy for you," she whispers into my ear.

"Yea, as much as my vagina needs a break, that was hot and I could really go again so I'm going to make a call." Pickle giggles as she pulls me in for a hug before smacking my ass and walking to the door.

I turn back to Grey, a wicked grin spread across my face.

"What are you thinking, Kitten?" He raises a brow at me.

I don't bother responding to him with words, instead dropping to my knees. I glance up at him through my lashes as I tug down his dark sweatpants, pleasantly surprised to find he's not wearing anything underneath. Freeing his thick, rock hard cock, I let out a moan in anticipation. My tongue juts over my dry lips, my mouth curling at the corners in a slight smirk before I lean forward, wrapping my hands around his thick thighs. Slowly dropping my mouth to the tip of his cock, I swipe my tongue against the bead of arousal waiting for me, his salty flavor exploding on my tongue.

His groans fill the room as I tease him, moving my hands from his thighs to grip the base of his cock, squeezing firmly with one as the other cups his balls, tugging gently. He takes a sharp breath as soon as he feels my lips wrap around his crown. I suck gently, pulling it into my mouth, still staring up at him.

"Fuck, Ry." He pants, his hands in fists at his sides. "Stop fucking teasing me, I need you to move. Fuck me with your hot little mouth."

I moan around him as I take him in deeper. His hands move to my head, fisting my hair, his fingers threading through my blond locks. I smile around his thick shaft as I pull back and sink him further into my throat. I slide my hand into my yoga pants, dipping my fingers between my slit, finding my own arousal dripping between my legs.

"Ry, are you touching yourself?" His voice is a deep growl with the question.

"Mmm" is all I'm able to articulate as my thumb grazes my clit. My own pleasure echoes around his cock. His resolve falters as soon as he hears my confirmation. His fists take stronger hold of my head as he thrusts into my throat.

"Fuck yourself while I fuck your mouth, babygirl." He groans.

I continue teasing my clit with my thumb, plunging my fingers inside my tight hole. I moan around him again as his thrusts become more erratic, my own release building in tandem with his. Tears fall down my face as he continues taking his own pleasure by fucking my face. I glide my thumb over the swollen bundle of nerves once more before I shatter around my own fingers.

"Yes, baby girl. Come with me." Before my brain can process the words, I taste his release as hot streams of come coat my tongue and throat. He stills as he fills my mouth, slowly pulling back and I flick my tongue against the sensitive tip as he removes himself from me. "Fucking hell, Ry. You're the most perfect woman alive." He moans as he pulls me onto my feet and frees the hand I used to make myself come from my pants. Bringing it up to his lips, he sucks my fingers into his mouth, licking clean the evidence of my orgasm.

Chapter Twenty

I've been splitting my time between packing up my dad's house and working at Nat's shop to give him a break. I'll be heading back to Miami for a few days to finish up the client I bailed on to come home, only giving me two more days here with Ryan. That thought makes me chuckle. I didn't think Central Falls would feel like home again but really, wherever Ryan is will feel like home. I've spent so much time fighting my feelings for her, I feel like a damn fool. The past week has been exhilarating. The creepy ass notes aside, being with her has been more than anything I could have ever imagined.

I just get done cleaning up after my latest session at Nat's when my phone dings with a text notification.

Ryan

> Hadley is going to pick me up from the studio. Meet us at Mud House?

Grey

> I'll head there as soon as I'm done cleaning up.

Ryan

> I miss you too.

I grin at her response. I don't know how I'm going to survive the distance when I have to go back to Miami. I groan as I finish the process of sanitizing my station.

Thirty minutes later I'm walking through the doors of Mud House. I see Pickle's teal hair first before Ryan comes into focus. The weather is cooler today which explains why she's wearing a cropped long sleeve t-shirt with another pair of yoga pants. The way she fills out her shirt leaves the soft skin along the underside of her breast exposed. My mouth dries at the sight. I close the distance between us, dragging her into my arms, my mouth crashing against hers with an urgent need. She moans softly into my mouth before pushing gently against my chest. I part my lips from hers, pressing my forehead against her shoulder. I don't release her, just breathing in her distinct scent, letting it wash over me.

"I really fucking like this top," I growl softly against her neck as I graze my finger tips under her breast. She shivers in my arms.

"I guess I'll need to wear only this for you at home then." I can feel her smile against my chest.

"Ok you two, break it up." Kayleigh groans from behind us, "Ry, I love you girl, but get a damn room."

Hadley erupts in laughter behind us. "Oh Kay, if you only knew how long I've been waiting for this to happen. I'm really surprised they've even come up for air long enough to grace us with their presence since they got their heads out of their asses."

"Mo Ghrá" I hear Connor's brogue cut through the laughter, the tone a clear admonishment.

Ryan turns to face the newcomer while still holding my waist.

"Baby!" Hadley squeals as she turns to see him heading towards us. She leaps into his arms as soon as he reaches her, wrapping her legs around his waist. They share a passionate kiss that puts Ryan and I to shame.

"Not you too." Kayleigh groans, attempting to hide her own laughter.

Connor gently places Hadley back on the ground and hugs Kayleigh. "How's my favorite girl?"

"Oh, she's a wild child. Both of the kids asked when you two were coming over again." She and Connor share a smile.

"We'll take them next weekend, you and Liam can enjoy some alone time," Hadley interjects. "I can't let my favorite man down."

I glance at Ryan in question. *Their kids,* she mouths. I nod in understanding before releasing her and stepping forward to shake Connor's hand.

"Nice to see you, man." I smile at him.

Ryan and I get back to her place after dinner. We're sitting on the couch with her tight little ass right at my cock and her back leaning against my chest. My arms are wrapped around her as we watch an episode of Gilmore Girls. She's seen this episode at least a hundred and one times. I'm absentmindedly running my hands up and down her forearms as the scene plays out before us: Collin and Logan burst into Rory's class at Yale while the Chilton student Rory is hosting sits next to her. They cause a scene, fake fighting, and before Finn comes in, wearing a British Bobby uniform, I pause the episode. She's mid laugh and turns around to face me.

"Listen, no matter how much I love a person, I will throw hands at anyone who interrupts this episode. Especially this scene!" she snarls. Honestly, it's adorable.

"Sorry, beautiful. But I need to ask you something." I chuckle.

She stiffens in my arms waiting for me to continue.

"I need to go back to Miami the day after tomorrow." Ry freezes at my words.

"You're leaving?" her voice is barely a whisper.

"I don't want to be away from you when I only need to be there for a few days," I give her a smirk, the one I know melts her and she relaxes back into me. "Come with me?"

"If I say yes, will you start this scene over from the beginning?" Her grin makes me chuckle.

"Anything for you, Kitten." At that, Ellie leaps onto Ry's lap and snuggles in for the re-watch and the rest of the episode.

Chapter Twenty-One

W e land at Miami International Airport at four a.m. Grey stands first and retrieves our bags from the overhead bin while I pick up a very angry Ellie from under my seat. She doesn't like flying, and apparently the tranquilizers Grey gave her before boarding must have worn off because she's currently howling in her crate.

After getting off the plane, we find our way to the exit where there is a line of taxis waiting to pick up travelers. Once we are seated safely in a taxi, I open the door to pet her. She calms down when she feels my hand caress her long silky fur. I smile up at Grey who is playfully glaring at me.

"I'm not sure how I feel about you commandeering my cat," he teases as he wraps an arm around my shoulders, pulling me against his chest. He presses a kiss against my forehead as we ride through the busy streets.

"How far is your shop from the beach?" I ask while watching the scenery change through the window.

"Two blocks, my condo is actually oceanfront. I'm on the 10th floor so we have a nice view." His lips twitch at the corner like he's fighting a smile.

"What aren't you telling me?" I raise a brow at him.

"You'll see in about," he glances out the window. "Four minutes."

I roll my eyes at him. There's no way he can be that precise. At least, I didn't think it was possible until I see we're pulling up to a stunning building, taller than some skyscrapers in NYC. I stare up at the tower of windows upon windows. The ocean air fills my senses, and I take a deep breath.

"Wow," I gasp, looking over at Grey who is opening his door and exiting the other side of the taxi. I open my door but before I can step out, Grey has already reached me, holding out a hand and pulling me from the taxi. I grab Ellie's carrier out of the back seat and turn back to face him. I grin up at the gorgeous man before me, "This is spectacular".

"You ready to see inside?" he asks.

It only took us four and a half hours to complete the *tour* of Grey's condo. He fucked me on every surface he could manage before I had to tap out. My body still hums two hours later sitting on the most comfortable couch I've ever had the pleasure of sitting on at Urban Ink, his tattoo shop. I make a mental note to ask where he bought it so I can get one for my studio.

He's been sketching at the desk while I'm scrolling through social media interacting with commenters. One of my favorite parts of the type of photography that I do is sharing it with people. The love and support I've received from strangers online is overwhelming. I've had several people travel to have sessions with me. It's been remarkable.

"Hey," I call out to Grey "Do you think your client would be ok with me photographing this? There was so much positive feedback on Hadley's pictures." I ask.

"I don't think he'd mind, Kitten. You can ask when he gets here." His lips curve into a lopsided grin that has me melting directly through the couch.

"So fucking unfair," I groan.

"What?" He feigns innocence, putting a hand on his chest. "I'm just looking at my girl."

"Mmhmm" is the only acknowledgment I give him before the door swings open and a tall, muscular man with spiky platinum hair walks in. His tanned arms are clearly covered in Grey's art.

"Wow, that's incredible," I say out loud before Grey even has a chance to say hello or introduce me to the guy.

"Hey, man." Grey chuckles, shaking his head, "Ry, this is Dylan. Dylan, Ryan," he introduces us.

"Ryan? THE Ryan? The one that you've been stalking on Instagram for as long as I've known you?" Dylan's eyes dart back and forth between the two of us.

"You've what?" I smirk at Grey.

"Oh shit, sorry man, I didn't mean to. Ah shit. I'm sorry." Dylan tries to cover for Grey and then gives up, realizing there's no coming back from outing his friend.

"Yea, I may have been keeping tabs on you. I missed you." Grey winks at me, closing the distance between us and pressing a soft kiss against my lips.

"You finally got her?" Dylan's excitement is contagious, as he slaps Grey on the shoulder in congratulations. "Yeah! Way to go man!"

Grey's face is bright red.

"Oh I'm totally not letting you off the hook that easily!" I giggle, slapping his chest playfully.

"Shit," Dylan groans imitating Picard's very memorable facepalm gif.

"Ok, D. Go get in my chair and quit making me look bad." Grey's throaty laugh sends a jolt of heat straight to my core. He playfully swats my ass before following after Dylan.

I follow after them to ask if Dylan minds that I photograph him. His response of "Fuck yeah!" has me pulling out my camera, and I spend the next several hours snapping pictures of the two of them. The intricate details that go into each of his pieces is breathtaking. Dylan tells me about each of the tattoos Grey's done for him which are most. They've been friends since he moved to Miami and Dylan has become a sort of human canvas for him, letting Grey take creative license with his designs. When they finally finish up, Dylan has a full color sleeve, and it's the most beautiful piece of art I've ever seen. The number of Marvel characters Grey was able to incorporate while keeping such incredible detail is astounding. The final piece was Captain America, which they did today. The way he was able to replicate the original comics for each of these characters has me at a loss for words. Seeing the final piece of the puzzle in place, I'm amazed at how incredibly talented Grey is.

Dylan apologizes to Grey again before we all say our goodbyes, making me laugh again. As Grey sanitizes his workstation, I pack up my camera.

"Are you hungry? I know a great restaurant a few blocks away," he calls from inside his room.

My stomach growls at the mention of food and I check the time. It's already seven p.m. and we haven't had anything since breakfast.

"Yes, please!" I pull my bag over my shoulder and walk towards his voice. "I'm famished."

"Oh, me too." He winks when he sees me, "but I'll save that for dessert."

Chapter Twenty-Two

The time in Miami went so fast, I barely had time to show Ryan around. She got a day on the beach though, which I may have enjoyed more than her. The sight of her in that tiny blue bikini, my dick never had a chance. After that we didn't leave the condo until it was time to come back home.

We're finally leaving the airport to head back to Ryan's place. Ellie is still angry over the plane ride, but I'm hoping she'll get used to it because I already know there's no way I'll be able to stay away from my girl.

"I can't wait to work on the pictures of you and Dylan." Ry muses next to me as she soothes Ellie with affection. She pulled Ellie out of the carrier as soon as we were all safely in my truck.

"I can't wait to see them. Every picture you've taken has been flawless." I squeeze her thigh.

"Oh don't think I forgot about that, sir," she laughs. "Just how long have you been *stalking* my socials?"

I wait a moment to respond, knowing it's either going to make or break us. I pull into her driveway and park before turning to face her.

"Since before I left." I swallow hard. "Ry, I've been in love with you for years but you're my best friend's little sister and you were too young."

Her eyes widen in shock.

"The apprenticeship...If it had come any later, even a year, I would have asked you to come with me." I pause. "You were only seventeen when I had to leave. I couldn't ask you to go, you were too young. Jack would have killed me."

"There's no way." She scoffs. "You couldn't have liked me for that long. You didn't even hug me until you were leaving."

"If I had touched you, felt you in my arms, against my body when I had no obligation to leave, I wouldn't have let you go." I barely breathe at the admission.

"You." Tears fill her eyes and my heart shatters. "What the fuck!" She screams but she's not looking at me. Her eyes are on her front door.

I turn, seeing something red on her front door.

"Stay here, call Bennett." I growl before I open the door and climb out of my truck. I close it behind me to make sure Ellie doesn't get loose.

I stalk closer to the front door to find; *you will be mine, soon.* Painted on the door in what I hope is red paint.

I don't go inside this time since I know my girls are safe. I walk back to the passenger side and open the door. Ryan is trembling, holding onto Ellie for dear life. I pull Ellie from her arms and place her back in the carrier before wrapping Ry in my arms in an attempt to calm her. She's safe and I won't let a damn thing happen to her.

"Kitten, it's ok," I whisper into her hair while I rub circles around her back.

"What does the door say, Grey?"

"Did you call Bennett?" I ask.

"Don't fucking change the subject. What does it say?" Her voice is so full of panic it makes my blood boil.

"It doesn't matter, babygirl. I won't let a damn thing happen to you." I echo my thoughts from a moment ago.

She pulls away from me to walk towards the door.

"Ry!" I call out after her.

She ignores me, of course.

"Who the fuck is doing this? Why now?" she cries when she sees the writing.

"It's ok. We'll figure it out."

That's a fucking promise. I won't rest until this nut job is just a bad fucking memory.

Bennett arrives at that moment, a handful of patrol cars with him.

"Ry, are you ok?" he asks as he approaches us.

"I'm tired of this Benny. Why is it getting worse?" she asks as she clings to me.

I reluctantly pry my eyes open, rolling over to see Ryan sitting with her back against the headboard and her knees pulled into her chest.

"What happened?" I ask as I sit up quickly, assessing my surroundings, and remember we stayed at Jack's last night.

"Nothing new. I just didn't get much sleep. Benny stayed over and they're louder than us," she groans.

I chuckle and pull her down, wrapping myself around her as we settle back into the warm sheets.

"I take that as a personal challenge," I smile before pressing my lips to her neck, sucking and licking her pulse point. My fingers dig into her hips as I grind my erection against her warm pussy. My hands travel up the length of her body, reaching the hem of her shirt. I tug it up, exposing her soft, toned stomach and perfect breasts. I softly run my fingers over my artwork and a shiver runs through her body. My mouth dips lower, tongue twirling around one pebbled peak and then the other. She whimpers at the soft touch. Knowing she needs more, I suck a nipple into my mouth, grazing my teeth against it just hard enough that the pain elicits a jolt of pleasure through her body. She moans my name into the room. I do the same to the other side gaining the same reaction. I smile up at her gorgeous face before trailing down her abdomen, alternating between soft kisses and nipping her silky skin.

"Grey." My name on her lips is a prayer for more, a request I will happily grant.

I hook my fingers into her sleep shorts and panties, pulling them over her hips and down her legs. I toss them to the floor and make myself at home between her gorgeous thighs. I plant soft kisses, nips and licks up her thighs. She writhes below me as I slowly travel to her core. I swipe my tongue slowly from her opening to her clit. Tasting her arousal first thing in the morning is my favorite way to start the day. She whimpers, begging for more.

"Oh baby girl. I think you can do better than that." I wink up at her as I glide a thick finger inside her drenched hole.

Ryan gasps at the intrusion and then moans when I reach her G spot. I insert another finger before returning my mouth to its feast. I continue pumping my fingers inside her, massaging her most sensitive spot as my tongue swirls around and flicks her clit. She's crying out and begging for me to make her come. I stop moving when I feel her pussy walls tightening around my fingers as she nears her climax . Raising my head to look up at her, I click my tongue.

"Not yet, beautiful. I want to hear you scream."

She groans when she sees the wicked grin spread across my face. I feel her pussy relax and dive back in to continue enjoying my treat. I continue edging her to several more orgasms before she screams in frustration.

"Make me come now, you psycho!"

I chuckle before I kneel between her legs, the tip of my cock at her entrance.

"I want you to scream so fucking loud for me that they hear you come in Denmark." I gaze into her eyes as I slide in at a slow, torturous pace. "Understood?"

"Yes, Fuck me. Make me come, Daddy!" she shouts out in frustration.

I smirk and thrust in to the hilt. She cries out at the sudden intrusion, and I wait for her to adjust but she digs her fingers into my forearms.

"If you don't fucking move," she cries out and it's all the invitation I need. I drive into her over and over, making sure I'm at an angle that the crown of my cock is hitting her G spot with each intrusion.

It takes less than a minute before she reaches her breaking point. Her already tight cunt strangles my cock as her crescendo sends her out of orbit. She screams and cries out in pleasure, louder than I've ever heard her before. She's clawing at my chest as I continue thrusting inside her several more times before I feel my balls tighten and pleasure ricochets through my body as I find my own release inside her.

I slowly pull out and pepper soft kisses along her body before my mouth crashes against hers. Her fingers curl into my hair as I swipe my tongue, parting her lips and opening her to me. She whimpers into the kiss, deepening it, as she grinds against my already stiffening cock. She pulls away slightly to catch her breath.

"More, Daddy!"

Chapter Twenty-Three

I just came for the fourth time around Grey's impressive dick when I hear Jack banging on the bedroom door.

"I swear, Grey. If you don't get off of my sister I'm going to come in there and beat the shit out of you."

"Come on, King." I hear Benny's deep chuckle, "I'm sure we kept them up last night. I'll make you coffee."

Jack's fading growl is the last thing I hear. Grey and I laugh for a moment before he pulls me out of bed and we walk to the connected bathroom.

After another quickie in the shower, Grey and I finally wash up. Forty-five minutes later, we're sitting around the kitchen table with Jack and Benny, drinking coffee.

"So," Benny breaks the silence. "Obviously whoever is stalking you has escalated. The concern now is the timing."

"What do you mean, timing?" I raise my brow at him.

"Grey comes home and y'all start getting closer." He doesn't bother to continue.

"You think it's because they think they're going to lose her to me?" Grey's voice cuts in as he pulls me closer to him.

"Yes." Benny says before bringing his coffee mug up to his lips, taking a large gulp.

"I don't understand, whoever it is would have never had me to begin with." I look between the three of them. "What does Grey have to do with it?"

"Because, sweetheart." Bennett's eyes soften. "While you may have only had eyes for Grey, they may have thought you were waiting for them since you haven't been with anyone for so long."

No one says anything as I burrow myself deeper into Grey's chest. If it were possible I'd be inside him with how close I've cuddled into him.

"I want you to think about something." Bennett's eyes meet Grey's this time and he pauses for a moment before continuing. "Go home."

From the way he raises his hands in defense, Grey and I both must have glared at him at the same time.

"I'm not saying stay gone. Come back and visit. It may give us time to figure out who's behind this. You being here is obviously escalating things too far. Our police department is too small to handle something like this so quickly," he explains.

"What if she comes with me?" Grey asks.

"I can't leave," I respond turning to him. "I enjoyed experiencing Miami with you but I don't want to stay there. This is my home. This is where I want to live."

"I know Kitten, and I will happily bring you back here. But, your safety is my priority." Grey's fingers brush against my jaw.

"I'm not leaving. They're not scaring me away from my home anymore than they already have," I yell at all of them.

I abruptly stand and storm out of the kitchen. I take the stairs two at a time to get back to the room Grey and I stayed in last night. Collapsing on the floor, I pull a sleeping Ellie into my lap, petting her purring body. I bury my face into her fur as the tears begin to flow.

"This isn't fair," I cry into her fur. I don't know how long I've been hiding in here with my feelings when I suddenly hear his deep timbre from the doorway.

"You know why I named her Ellie?" Grey's voice startles me. I look up to see him leaning against the door frame.

Why is he so damn beautiful?

"No, why?" I look up at him from under wet lashes.

"Your middle name." He smiles shyly at me, closing the distance between us. He stands in front of me, bending down to pick me up from the floor before sitting me on the bed.

"What?" I ask, the revelation making my mind spin.

"Beautiful. If they think the best option is for me to go back to Miami for a bit I will come back here every fucking week. Ellie will start earning her own frequent flyer miles with how often I will come back to you." He presses a kiss against my forehead, breathing me in. "I don't fucking like this but my priority is your safety and if they tell me that it's the best way to keep you safe, we'll figure it out."

I wrap my arms around his waist and he holds me against him for a moment before dropping to his knees. He takes my chin between his fingers, raising my gaze to meet his. He stares into my eyes for a long moment before his voice finally cuts through the silence.

"I love you, Ryan." His confession breaks me all over again.

Chapter Twenty-Four

We've been doing long distance dating for two months. The stalker hasn't made much of an attempt in contacting me since I took Grey to the airport. True to his word, he's been visiting every week with Ellie.

I think she's starting to resent me.

Do cats resent people?

I have been staying back at my place, after having a security system and cameras installed. Benny insisted before they would all agree to let me leave Jack's. Kat and Hadley have been staying over on occasion, but I hate pulling them from their lives. Hadley and Connor are nearly inseparable, I don't know how she's able to pry herself away from him to be here for me. Don't get me wrong, I'm grateful, but they're gross with how in love they are.

Maybe I'm jealous because I don't have that constantly.

No. I am jealous. I fucking miss him. I had him for just over a month before he was torn away from me by this fucking stalker. I know he wouldn't have moved here but we didn't even get to have a conversation about what we wanted. Hairy donkey balls! I couldn't even respond when he confessed his feelings for me.

I've been sitting at the studio for hours staring at my computer, attempting to edit the shoot from yesterday, but I can't concentrate. I finally give up, opening Instagram instead. The pictures I posted of Grey and Dylan's session are still going wild. Every day someone else comments on them.

@IngridsPerfection You're so good!
@Paddlebaby damn, @GreysInk. Your work is amazing.
@MRVL4lyfe Just now seeing these! They look awesome! Thanks for capturing the process @RySnaps It was great meeting you! Take care of my boy!

I smile at Dylan's response. Before I can respond, my phone dings with a text notification.

Grey

You busy, Kitten?

Never too busy for you. What's up?

I barely hit send before the phone rings with a FaceTime request. I chuckle to myself, shaking my head as I answer.

"Hey." I smile at the phone as I stare at Grey's delicious features on my screen. He's outside but the camera is so close to his face I can't see what he's doing.

"Hey, Babygirl." He sighs, "I miss you."

"I miss you too. Have I mentioned I really fucking hate this?" I pout.

"I know, trust me. I know." His smile turns sad.

"What's wrong?" I ask, my heart drops to my stomach as I wait for a response.

"I think Ellie is mad at me," he groans into the phone.

I stand from my seat at the desk and giggle as I walk toward the back where my refrigerator is.

"And why would she ever be mad at you?" I open the door to the fridge and pull out a bottle of water. Before Grey can respond, I hear the bell for my studio door open.

"Oh, I need to go. Someone just walked in. I'll call you back in a bit." I blow a kiss before disconnecting the call and jog to the lobby. When I enter the room, Grey is standing in front of me, a sly grin pulling at his lips, Ellie's carrier on the ground next to him.

"Oh my god!" I squeal less than a second before I leap onto him, wrapping my legs around him and hanging on to him like the koala I become any time we're reunited.

His arms snake around my back, holding me against him. Our lips crash together, his tongue parting my lips as he enters my mouth, fucking it with the need we both feel. I moan into him, grinding my core against his hard length. He groans at the friction before pulling away. He presses his lips to my neck just below my ear sending shockwaves through my system.

"Hi, Kitten," he whispers before lowering me back to the ground.

"What are you doing here? I thought you weren't coming back for a few more days?" I lace my fingers in his as he picks up Ellie's carrier and we walk back to the dressing room I have for clients. I sit on the couch as he closes the door and joins me. I open the carrier and Ellie immediately emerges and jumps onto my lap for snuggles. I run my fingers through her long silky fur while staring at Grey.

"I had something come up that I will have to leave early for and I didn't want to miss out on any time with you." He smirks. "I'm content just hanging out here while you do shoots. I can sketch in your office and stay out of the way when you have clients here."

"Luckily for me, I was actually going to just force Hadley and Kat into some impromptu hiking shoots, so I'm all yours." I grin, tugging on the collar of his shirt to bring him closer to me for another kiss while not disturbing Ellie.

The few days Grey was with me went by too quickly, as they always seem to. I'm just leaving the airport drop-off again. Saying goodbye, even for a little while, is so painful.

I press the call button on my steering wheel and initiate a call to Hadley. The line rings three times before she answers.

"Hey Ry, what's up?" She sounds so chipper.

"I'm just leaving the airport." I sigh into the phone, holding in the tears.

"Oh, babe. Do you want to go for coffee? Or maybe something stronger?" Her cheer dissipates when she realizes I'm hurting.

"Can I just come over?" I sigh, "I don't want to be around people."

"Sure, I'll call Kat and have her bring coffee. I already have Bailey's and whiskey here." She giggles.

"Thank you. See you soon." I disconnect the call and drive, turning left out of the airport toward Connor and Hadley's house.

I've been driving for less than five minutes when the tears start falling. I should be used to this by now. We've been doing this for months, but I always have the same visceral reaction. Sobs wrack through my body, so I pull off to the side of the road, the best I can, being surrounded by woods on either side. I'm not sure how long I've been sitting here when a soft knock on my window startles me. I wipe my eyes and see an oddly familiar face. Where do I know her from? Her lips turn into a warm smile when she recognizes me. I press the button on my door to lower my window.

"Hey! Are you ok?" she asks as if we've known each other for years.

"Yea, my boyfriend just left to go home, and my emotions got the best of me for a bit. I'll be ok." I give her a small smile that doesn't reach my eyes.

"Oh, I didn't realize." Her lips turn down into a scowl.

I look back out of the windshield, about to tell her I should go, but before I have a chance, I feel a cloth covering my mouth and nose. The strong smell of chemicals fills my nose. I try to pull at her hand, but the more I struggle, the harder I breathe, sending the fumes straight to my brain. My surroundings start to become fuzzy just before everything goes dark.

Chapter Twenty-Five

Jack

I knew this would happen. She's constantly crying, a fucking mess each time he leaves. My baby sister has been a hard ass since our mom died, so for this relation-shit, because that's what it is, to be affecting her so much, that every time he flies off she's in tears and needs to drink in order to cope, has me seeing red. I'm fucking done letting him get away with this shit. It may have been Bennett's idea to go back to Miami, but I know Greyson can keep her safe here in Central Falls.

I step off of the plane onto the tarmac, having taken the smallest plane known to man - ok, I'm exaggerating, just a little - it's too small to use a tunnel. The overwhelming humidity makes beads of sweat roll down my forehead and neck from the brief exposure. I only brought a backpack of clothing and I'm fairly certain I am going to need some shorts. It's hotter than I expected here, jeans aren't going to cut it. I take a few steps forward until a sign catches my eye directing me to enter the airport in order to exit. Of course I'm at a D gate so nowhere near where I need to be. I toss my pack over my shoulder and start walking. Once I reach the door, I pull it open, welcoming the cool breeze.

Thank you, Willis Carrier.

The taxi is finally pulling up to Greyson's building forty-five minutes later. I open the door and step out, thanking the driver before dragging my bag onto my back once more.

Jesus. This man has done well for himself if he's living here.

I walk inside the building looking around at how bright and shiny everything is. I would get incredibly distracted living in a place like this. I find the elevator after a few moments of wandering around. I press the call button and it opens almost immediately. I step in and turn toward the bank of buttons, thankful my protective nature had me snagging Greyson's address from the driver's license the last time he was in town and left his wallet unattended in my kitchen. I press the button for the tenth floor. I lean back against the cool metal while the numbers increase at a snail's pace.

I just want to get this over with so he either comes back with me or ends it for good.

A ding indicating I arrived sounds just before the doors open. I step off of the elevator and turn in the direction of his condo. As I approach, the door opens and a big-breasted blonde comes strutting out like she's on a goddamn runway. She turns to him, brushing her hand against his forearm and leaning in close before speaking. My feet start moving on their own accord, stopping just a few feet from them.

"Are you fucking kidding me, Greyson?" I roar.

Both he and boobs have a look of shock on their faces.

"What are you doing here, brother?" His question just pisses me off.

"Don't 'brother' me. I told you I would fucking kill you." I snarl, taking another step toward him.

"Whoa, Jack. It's not like that. Dumbass." He shakes his head, a chuckle passing his lips. Rage rips through my veins at his flippant attitude. I'll rip his goddamn dick off for fucking around on my sister. I advance on him again, but he holds up his hands to stop me.

"This is Tonya. She's my realtor." His lips pull into a satisfied grin as I come to a halt with my arm wound back ready to unleash my anger.

She's his *what?*

Chapter Twenty-Six

Seeing Jack standing in front of me with a look of confusion on his face is one of the best things I've seen during our entire friendship. He's glancing back and forth between Tonya and me, unable to grasp what's happening. It's taking all of my self control not to double over in laughter.

"I'm selling my condo, asshole." I chuckle and Jack slowly lowers his arm.

"You're what?" His face twists into a shocked expression.

"I'm moving back to Central Falls. I'm tired of not being with Ry every day so we can deal with shit together. I was planning on surprising her in a few days once everything is packed up and ready to go. That's why I came back this morning." I can't help but grin as his eyes go wide.

"Oh, thank fuck. I was ready to kill you both." He groans, scrubbing a hand down his face.

"Uh. I'm gonna go, Mr Mancini," Tonya stutters. "I'll be in touch when we have a buyer for both locations." Tonya takes a wide step around Jack, looking incredibly nervous.

"He won't hurt you, he's my girlfriend's big brother and takes the protective detail a little too far sometimes." I shake my head.

"I'm really sorry, my brain hadn't quite caught up with the situation. I really wouldn't hurt you." Jack holds his hands up in surrender.

Tonya doesn't respond, just waves back at us as she retreats to the elevator.

"Come on in, dumbass," I chuckle as I move aside for him to go into my place.

He walks past me and into my space. Without a word, he crosses the open floorplan to my couch and takes a seat, waiting for me to join him. I shake my head, a soft chuckle passing my lips as I take a seat across from him in the arm chair.

"So, you're really doing this?" He asks, his voice low.

"Yes. She may not have told me she loves me, but I know she does." I smile at the memory of the joy in her eyes when I confessed my feelings for her. "She's afraid I'll leave and I want to prove to her the only way I'm leaving this relationship is in a body bag."

"Ok. Fine." He pulls out his phone and types something out before sliding it back into his pocket as his lips twitch into a soft smile. "Let's get packing, I want to get back to my man too."

We spend the next three days loading things into boxes. It concerns me that Ryan hasn't responded to any of my messages over these past few days. It's super out of character for her, but I try not to let that bring me down, knowing she has a hard time when I leave.

I purge things that won't be necessary back home. We don't have a beach or ocean in Central Falls so my surfboard can definitely be re-homed. When we finally get my condo packed up–with the exception of Ellie–on the third morning, Jack and I venture out to my tattoo studio.

We take the short walk from my building to my shop. Opening the door and taking a step inside, the first thing I see is one of my artists, Niall, sitting on the couch watching The Great British Baking Show. Smiling, I shake my head. This is where he always is if he doesn't have a client. His long, dirty blonde hair is pulled back in tight viking braids. His muscular arms covered in elaborate ink are on full display, the tight white wife beater shirt now hiding much of his physique.

"Oh, what episode are you on?" Jack asks as soon as he sees the TV, before Niall realizes he's not alone.

"Fuck man!" He jumps to his feet, holding his hand to his chest. "Make a noise next time asshole!" He glares at me before looking at Jack. His eyes soften when he responds, "Series eleven, the pastry episode, I just started it a few minutes ago if you want to join me?"

Jack's face turns crimson at Niall's obvious eyefucking. I clear my throat, bringing the attention back to me.

"Yea, we're not going to have time for that today, Are C and Loki here?" I ask.

"Yea, they're in Lo's room, what's up?" Niall's eyebrow raises nearly to his hairline.

"Give me a minute and we'll all talk," I say as I walk toward the back of the studio. I knock on the door to Loki's room. "Put your dick away, C. I need you both up front now," I call through the door, hearing an exasperated "Fuck" through the wall.

I walk back up and lean against the counter, waiting for the others. Jack and Niall are talking about the show and Jack is going on about how he doesn't have a favorite episode but is obsessed with the entirety of the 2018 season.

After a few moments, I hear Loki's door open, and they walk out, heads down like they are a couple of kids with their hands caught in the cookie jar.

"I don't give a shit if y'all fuck as long as no one is here. Just don't be stupid about it." I roll my eyes knowing damn well I have no room to speak considering the first time I took Ry was inside of Alchemy Ink. "That's not why I wanted you two out here," I continue.

Niall stands, ready to interrupt me, but I put my hand up, motioning for him to wait.

"I'm moving back to Central Falls, effective immediately." Lo's hand goes to their mouth, their eyes showing the shock they're feeling as I continue. "I'm not closing the shop here and I will come back occasionally. However, if one or all of you are at a point that you'd like to buy me out together we can talk terms."

"Ryan?" C asks as he rubs a hand over his shaved scalp a sly smile on his face as he wraps an arm around Loki's waist.

"Of course. Her brother Jack even came to help me pack so I could get back sooner to surprise her." I grin back at him.

"I'm so happy for you, boss man, but shit. I'm gonna miss you!" Lo says as they run toward me, wrapping their arms around me. Long, pink, just-fucked hair tickles my nose a second before they pull away. I barely hold back a chuckle.

"Thanks, kid. Now, if any of you need anything while we're figuring out next steps, please reach out. I'm only a call away and if I need to come back for anything, I will." C steps forward to pull Loki away as he and I shake hands.

Niall is the last one to move. "I have been telling you to go back home since I met you, Your heart was always back there with her, man." His wide grin warms my heart. "Congrat's, dude." He pulls me in for a half hug, patting my shoulder before backing away.

After a few hours of back and forth, we've hammered out the specifics of how the shop is going to run while I'm gone, or at least until they determine if they want to buy me out. We finish up and Jack and I are finally ready to say goodbye. Lo wraps me in another embrace before C pulls them off of me chuckling. Loki has always been emotional and hates goodbyes, so I expected this reaction when I dropped the news on them today.

Jack and I head back out into the June heat and walk a block south to a restaurant to grab take out. We're chatting for a bit as we eat, Jack telling me more about Bennett and how they met. While the visit may have started off on a sour note, the past few days of reconnecting with my best friend have been something I will cherish forever. Finally finishing our lunch, we make our way back to my condo. Packing the remaining items of Ellie's, I put her on her harness and leash so she can walk out on her own like the proper lady she is instead of being shoved into a carrier. We place the few things of hers in the back of the U-haul before climbing in the cab. Jack settles into the passenger seat and takes Ellie from me when I pull myself up into the driver side.

As I pull away from what has been my home and city for the last few years, I feel a weight lifting from my chest.

I'm pulling onto the highway just as Jack's phone rings. He smiles, and I know it's one of two people calling. I'm putting my money on Bennett with how big the smile is though. Sure enough, he swipes at the screen before bringing the phone to his ear.

"Hey baby, we're on our way ho—" He doesn't finish the sentence when I notice his face fall. He goes white as a ghost a second later. "How long?" he asks.

I can't make out the other end of the conversation, my heart is pounding so hard it may turn into a chestbuster.

"Do you have any leads?" Jack's voice is low, and he's holding back tears. I haven't heard that kind of emotion since his mom passed away.

No, I shake the thought from my head. Absolutely not.

"It's going to be a few days before we get back home. It's a twenty-nine hour drive" His voice cracks as he speaks.

"What the fuck is going on," I interupt him before my imagination conjures up anything worse than it already has.

"Pull over." Jack looks at me before he goes back to the conversation. "I'll call you when we have an ETA. I love you, baby."

I pull over, putting the truck into park, staring at Jack while I wait for an answer.

"She's missing. Her car and phone were found a mile from the airport the day we left."

His words hit me with the force of a Mack truck.

Chapter Twenty-Seven

She thought she could trick me by having him travel back and forth? She can't be that dense. Not my girl. Someone else must have put that idea in her pretty little head. I smile at her sleeping form from the doorway, her bare breasts rising and falling with each breath she takes and her beautiful skin on full display. I'll give the man one thing, he knows how to tattoo. The cardinal on her ribcage is the most beautiful piece of art I've seen on skin.

We're really lucky we had a bit of time to get this set up, with the game they were playing. It's really perfect for what I have in mind. At least until she understands that she belongs to me.

"She really is a stunner. I understand why you want her so badly, Ing," My boyfriend, Travis, says from behind me, his front pressing against my back. I groan as I feel his thick cock stiffening against my ass.

"Listen, babe. I told you you could fuck me while I have fun with her. I've always wanted to have a threesome with you," I purr as I tilt my head back onto his chest and he trails his fingers up my sides, caressing the delicate skin along the sides of my breasts.

"Then what are you waiting for?" he whispers into my neck as he slaps my ass.

I giggle before stepping forward, pulling off the shorts and tank top I kept on while I tried to wait patiently for her to wake. Now, I've lost my patience, it's time for me to enjoy my meal.

I pick up the leather gloves I set just out of reach from her, pulling them on one at a time. I turn towards Travis who hands me the knife I chose, especially for her. I unfold the blade from the curved handle. The end is rounded, something I know she'll enjoy once we get started. I drop to my knees in front of my beautiful girl and crawl between her luscious thighs, pressing soft kisses up each side before pressing my nose between her pussy lips, inhaling her scent.

Chapter Twenty-Eight

I feel a set of soft lips and a warm tongue lapping at my cunt. I groan, unable to open my eyes and fully appreciate Grey between my legs. I'm so tired and my body feels heavy. My mind is clouded with unclear memories as I continue struggling to find consciousness. I hear a soft, feminine moan just before something cold and hard slides inside my pussy. With adrenaline pulsing through my veins, my eyes fly open and

I look down between my legs, pulling at my arms only to realize I'm chained to a pole in a dark and dank cellar.

"What the fuck!" I try to scream but it comes out a moan. I look between my legs to find the same girl from before eating my pussy. My heart lurches in my chest. I try to buck and move her away from me.

"Stop!" I scream as the hard cold thing enters my pussy again sliding in at a curve until something smooth hits my skin.

"Who the fuck are you?" I cry out as she attaches herself to my clit, sucking in the most amazing rhythm. "Oh my god, stop!" I sob, but she continues her assault as if she can't hear my screams.

A naked man walks up behind her, a dark look in his eyes, his hand is wrapped around his hard dick as he moves closer to us. My eyes close as tears fall.

Please let this be a nightmare.

"You ready, Ing?" His voice is hoarse with lust.

My eyes open wide, terrified of what he's asking. The girl between my legs reaches behind her, never pulling away from my cunt to motion him forward. He lines himself up behind what I now notice is her bare ass before slamming his cock inside her. She moans against my clit, all while continuing to suck at the same rhythm, still fucking me with the same unknown object.

He thrusts inside her for several minutes before looking over her body at me. "She's not coming until you do." He winks, a cruel smile playing on his lips.

My stomach convulses, and I squeeze my eyes shut again.

The girl, Ing, laps at my clit again alternating between licks and sucks while the curved thing hits my G-Spot. Unable to fight it any longer, I climax, my screams filled with a mixture of pleasure, pain and terror. Immediate guilt washes over me as my stomach twists around itself, what just occurred replaying in my mind. I lurch and jerk against the chains as the contents of my stomach expel from my mouth all over my naked body and the mattress.

I sob as the man finds his release in her and she finally releases herself from me. I squeeze my legs shut the best I can, realizing they're chained at both sides at the foot of the mattress.

"Let me go! Who are you? Why are you doing this to me? Let me go!" I scream out at them both.

"It hurts that you don't recognize me, gorgeous" She pouts before winking at me.

Chapter Twenty-Nine

I haven't slept for thirty hours by the time we arrive home. Jack and I took turns driving the entire way, breaking a multitude of traffic laws. My emotions have been a mess, ranging from fear to rage since Bennett's call. I'm thankful I wasn't alone otherwise I don't know how the fuck I would have made it back here. As we pull the U-Haul up to Jack's house, Bennett, Hadley, Kat and Connor are standing on the front porch waiting for us. Jack carries Ellie since the two of them have become obnoxiously close during the drive. Jack walks toward Bennett who embraces him and presses a kiss to his forehead. Hadley releases Connor and runs up to me wrapping her arms around me, sobbing. I hold her close for a moment before she pulls away.

"What do you know?" I direct the question to Bennett.

"She pulled off on Log Road in a secluded area. There aren't any cameras back there." He pauses. "The last communication we have is her calling Hadley after you left."

Hadley's sobs become audible, Kat and Connor wrap their arms around her in an attempt to comfort her.

"You told me to fucking leave," I bark at Bennett. "You told me she'd be safer if I fucking left. This is your fucking fault!" I point at him, rage coating each word. "I swear to whatever fucking god you believe in, if anything happens to her I will fucking end you, motherfucker," I snarl.

Bennett flinches as I walk forward. I take Ellie from Jack's arms and walk into the house heading straight upstairs. I put her down on the bed I've used when staying here, before quickly grabbing the rest of her things to make sure she's comfortable. I walk back downstairs to find everyone sitting in Jack's living room.

Hadley looks up at me with tears in her eyes.

"Greyson, what are we gonna do?" Her voice is weak.

I don't respond. I can't. I'm too fucking scared to say anything to her. I glance at Jack and Connor.

"Let's go." Connor stands and joins me. Jack hesitates, looking at Bennett. "She's your fucking sister." I snarl.

Jack doesn't say anything as he stands to join us.

"Bennett, you can either come with us to find something or you can stay out of my fucking way because when I find this motherfucker, I'm ending them." I glare at him before walking out the front door.

I'm at Ry's desk at her photography studio looking for anything that might help us find her, while Bennett stands behind me doing absolutely nothing helpful. I open her laptop and enter the pin, my birthday. I open it to see her Instagram feed pulled up with five new notifications, all for separate posts.

Under a photo of Ry and I at the beach.

@IngridsPerfection *It breaks my heart that you think you can stay away from me*

One I took of Ry laying on my bare chest before we came back to Central Falls.

@IngridsPerfection *I can't help wonder what you'd feel like*

A picture from when I first came home, before we even started dating.

@IngridsPerfection *You're supposed to be mine*

A candid she took of me with the caption, *I've always been yours.*

@IngridsPerfection *Liar*

The photo we took of us kissing before I left this last time.

@IngridsPerfection *He can't have you*

"What the fuck," I growl looking over my shoulder at Bennett who looks mortified. "You didn't bother checking her fucking social media?"

He doesn't respond to me, just pulls his phone out of his pocket, making a call.

"I want the entire fucking department here, now. They were supposed to have gone through all of her things. Why the fuck are we finding this now? She's the closest thing I have to a sister and y'all are treating the case like it's a joke," he spews through the phone.

I keep staring at the screen. I click on the profile to see photo after photo of the same figure. It's a woman, she's got a killer body but no face is shown in any of the pictures. I pull my phone from my pocket to call Kat knowing Hadley won't be able to talk.

"Hello?" she whispers into the phone, her voice sounding so broken.

"Is everything ok?" My heart stutters in my chest and I hold in a breath afraid something else has happened.

"Yea, Hadley fell asleep, What's up?" she asks and I release my breath.

"We found something but I'm not sure what it is. I'm going to send you an Instagram link. Tell me if you recognize anything." I send the link and she goes quiet as she pulls the phone from her ear to look at the screen. After a long moment, she gasps. "I recognize this lingerie. Go back a month or two on Ryan's posts. She did a shoot using that set. I'm not sure if it's the same person but it's not a set I've seen very often."

I scroll back on the computer looking for the same thing the Ingrid person is wearing and I come across an image Ryan posted not long after I first arrived. Same lingerie set, same body.

"I've gotta go, thanks Kat." I disconnect the call before she has a chance to respond.

"Bennett, look at this." I bring the two pictures side by side.

"What the fuck?" It's all he says before a handful of people wearing CFPD uniforms walk into the studio.

Chapter Thirty

I've been staring at my tablet for the last five hours, flipping back and forth between Ry's account and Ingrid's account, willing something to happen, for any insight on where she is. After the police department got here, they told me I needed to give them access to what I've been looking at. I handed over Ryan's computer reluctantly, since they were worthless from the onset of all that's happened. Bennett's insistence and guarantee that he would bring her home was the driving force behind me handing it over.

I groan into my hands when I feel a hand on my shoulder.

"We're gonna find her, because I'm not going to let Hadley get hurt again." Connor's thick brogue cuts through the silence where I've been isolating myself.

I break at his words. "I just got her, man. I can't lose her." The unshed tears finally break free, flooding down my face.

Connor pulls me up into a tight embrace, letting me know without words that I'm not alone in this. I sob into his shoulder for several moments before a ding sounds from my tablet, pulling me back into the here and now. I jerk away to see the notification. A new post from the Ingrid account, a caption on an up close photo of Ryan's tattoo.

@IngridsPerfection *Don't worry, I'll take good care of her.*

"Jaysus," Connor spits out from beside me.

Another ding chimes and I reload the page to another image, this time of Ryan's hands chained around a pole.

I can't speak. I can barely breathe as I look at the caption.

@IngridsPerfection *I don't think she's going to miss you once I've had my fun with her.*

I stand up lifting the desk and throwing it against the wall. It smashes into pieces at the impact.

"I'm gonna kill this motherfucker!" I roar as I storm outside.

"Mr. Mancini," a police officer approaches me as soon as I exit the building.

"What?" I snarl at him.

"There is new information we wanted to discuss." His response is low.

"Unless the information is you know where she is and you're bringing her home right now, I don't want to fucking hear it." I glare at him before he takes a step back and nods.

My phone notification goes off in my pocket. I pull it out to find an incoming video call from a number I don't have saved in my phone. I swipe the green button to answer it.

"Hello?" I say holding the phone in front of my face, Connor having joined me at my side. I hear shuffling and soft whimpers through the call.

"Please let me go. I don't want this, Luna. Please. Let me go." The screen cuts to a set of chocolate eyes full of so many different emotions. I hear the rattling of chains, and before the screen jerks, I catch a glimpse of something familiar as I hear Ryan vomiting.

"She's mine now," a feminine voice whispers before the call drops.

Blood boils through my veins as I walk to my truck across the parking lot. Connor jogs behind me.

"What's going on?" He grabs my shoulder trying to pull me to a stop.

"I know where they are and I'm fucking ending this since the police department is worthless," I snarl. "Either join me or keep them off my tail."

We step into the back yard and I take in the familiar sight. Before I left I really thought we could make this ours. Now If I never see my childhood home again, it will be too fucking soon.

I point to Connor to check the other side of the house and motion for him to meet me around front.

It only takes a few minutes before we're both at the front with no sign of life inside. Praying to whatever gods are listening that we get in there without alerting anyone to our entry I wave my hand toward him, motioning that he follow me. I carefully twist the handle, thankful that it's unlocked.

Keep breathing, you almost have her back.

I push the door open an inch at a time to make sure no one is around, taking in my childhood living room. I hear Ryan's muffled screams from downstairs when the basement door opens and a man I've never seen before comes rushing out toward me. I ball my hands into fists before I wind back and start whaling on the stranger in front of me. My fists connect with his skin over and over again until I feel his bones cracking under the weight of my punches. When he finally stops moving, I let out a long breath and stand only to realize I'm covered in his blood. Connor is standing, staring at me before his eyes flick to the ground. A few feet from the stranger lies a gun he must have dropped during our rumble. I pick it up and look back at Connor.

"Stay here, make sure he doesn't move. And call Bennett." I mouth to him just before I disappear down the stairs.

Chapter Thirty-One

My tongue is flicking her clit, lapping up the arousal I've caused from my touch, my mouth. Her taste is the sweetest thing to ever grace my tastebuds. She's screaming for me to stop, but if she really wanted me to she wouldn't be coming around the handle of my blade every time I fuck her. I stare up at her as she begs and pulls on her chains, her chocolate brown eyes burning into my soul. It takes me back to the first time I saw her.

2 years ago

I open the door of Travis' F150 and hop down. He rounds the bed of the truck to meet me and take my hand in his. I lean into him, breathing in his familiar scent of amberwood and sage when I look up toward the entrance of Ignite and see the most stunning woman. Her blond hair is pulled up in a high ponytail, and she's in a mini dress that barely covers her ass. My mouth waters at the sight of her. Mm, I bet she tastes divine.

I notice two women standing with her, one heavier than the other who has a large chest. Though all three are attractive, the blonde has my full attention. We begin to walk closer to the entrance and I see the one with a nice rack embrace *my* woman. I glare in their direction when the one holding her says something loud enough for me to hear.

"Ryan, can I stay with you tonight?" My girl nods her head yes. So her name is Ryan. *Good to know.* I file the information away for later.

Over the time I've been watching her, she's never stayed in a relationship for more than a few weeks, and even then, it's usually a one night stand. Her only constant has been the two women I saw her with that first night. Although the heavier one has brought a man into the group that has gotten close to all of them in one way or another.

I've left notes for her which she never seems to appreciate. I've even left her flowers a few times, but she throws them away. I can't understand why she's pushing me away like this. Even Travis understands that I belong to her now. He and I may still be involved sexually, but he knows my heart belongs to her.

I'm sitting in my usual spot at Mud House when a man walks up behind her. The friend I've learned is named Hadley greets him with much excitement that my Ryan doesn't share. She goes rigid, her eyes flickering with so much emotion. Rage boils through my veins as I watch the scene before me.

I need to take her soon.

I pull on the long raven colored wig, covering my naturally golden locks, making sure it's glued in place before I dress. The red lingerie set is something I found from a tiny local boutique several towns away and it perfectly shows off what I'm offering up to Ryan. The strap around my neck is the collar that holds the tether to the beautiful blonde I'm about to officially meet.

I stand by the door of her studio waiting for her arrival. I know I'm early but I need the extra time with her. I feel her presence before I look up to see her standing in front of me with a hesitant smile on her face.

"Hi! I'm Ryan, may I help you?" she asks as she takes a few steps toward me.

"Oh, hi! I'm Luna. I'm you're one o'clock session. I just got here a little early and since it's so nice I didn't want to wait in my car." I grin at her.

She leads me inside to a room where I can get changed. It doesn't take me long since I wore the lingerie beneath my clothes. Once everything I don't want in these photos is set down neatly on the couch, I take a step out into the hall. She's bent over her bag in the lobby, her perfect ass on display. It takes everything in me not to grab it and knead the soft flesh. I quietly walk up behind her to get a better look at her beautiful physique.

The moment she calls me 'gorgeous,' I know she feels the same attraction I do. The need to be together. She's just afraid to admit it.

Present day

I feel her body trembling under my touch and the languid strokes of my tongue against her clit, my blade handle reaching her inner most sensitive spot. Glancing up, I can see the tears streaming down her beautiful face as she cascades over the edge and I take her release again.

I sit up on my knees to watch her come down from her high. It's beautiful, until she vomits. Again. That part's gross; I don't understand why she reacts this way when she obviously enjoys what I do to her.

Her body convulses and jerks against the chains as she expels the contents of her stomach yet again.

"You know you enjoy me, Ryan. Why do you keep reacting this way when I make you feel so good?" I ask, a snark in my voice I can't help.

Before I can continue, I feel a large hand around my throat and a hard body behind me. Not the one I expect, either. I stiffen at the intruder.

Chapter Thirty-Two

I feel her stand from the mattress and I close my legs as tight as I can with the restraints still attached when I hear it. The voice I've been dreaming of, that I've been praying for since this began. My eyelids shoot open, taking him in.

"I swear to fucking god, you bitch. If you move I will kill you where you stand." Grey's command is thick with rage. "Where are the keys?"

"Like I'll fucking tell you." Luna or Ingrid - I don't know anymore - snarls back at him. "She's mine. You were never supposed to touch her. She's always been mine!" I see her hand attempting to turn the knife around so she can palm the handle instead of the blade.

"Knife!" I scream as loud as my tender throat will allow.

Grey drops his free hand to the arm with the knife, squeezing her wrist so tightly it drops on the ground before he kicks it away.

"Take me to the fucking keys," he growls as he squeezes her throat.

She wheezes out a breath while pointing toward the opposite side of the stairs. Wrapping his arm around her torso, his hand still gripping her throat, he carries her in the direction she pointed. He puts her down in front of him and grabs a ring of keys from the wall. He continues gripping her throat so hard she begins to paw and scratch at his hand to be released. He grips the back of her head before letting go and slams her face into the cement wall in front of them. She collapses to the ground and he comes rushing toward me. A loud sob erupts from my throat and echoes around the room.

"Oh, baby, I'm so sorry. I'm so, so sorry." Grey's face is twisted with guilt as he works to release me.

He leans over me, his hands on the cuffs at my wrists. I hear a click before my arms drop free. I bring them to my chest, rubbing each wrist. He works quickly, moving down to my feet, unlocking the first cuff when I see movement out of the corner of my eye.

"Grey!" I scream. He turns around with that gazelle-like quickness, pulling a gun from the back of his waistband, aiming it at where Luna is standing.

"You can't keep me away from her," she snarls through the blood dripping down her face.

"Stay the fuck away from me, you psychopath!" I cry.

"It's ok, baby. She won't touch you again." Grey's voice rushes over me like a blanket of calm. "Close your eyes, beautiful."

I do as he asks, squeezing my eyes shut, praying and begging to any god that will listen that this ends now.

"You think you can hurt me? I'm a woman, no one will believe you." Her voice is so shrill a dog barks not far off in the distance in response.

I hear a click less than a second before a loud bang sounds so close, my ears begin to ring. A loud thud startles me, my eyes shooting open to see Grey still in the same position, I look to where Luna was standing only to see her lying on her stomach, unmoving. Her face is in my line of sight and her eyes are still on me, but I can see the emptiness in them.

Grey stands up quickly, unlocking the last cuff before wrapping me in the blanket that my captors would throw over me when they were done with me. He lifts me in his arms and takes the stairs two at a time until we're in a familiar room.

"What?" I ask as I look around taking in my surroundings. "Why did they bring me here?" I cry, clinging onto Grey's neck.

"Ryan!" I hear Connor's voice through the haze.

I look behind Grey to see Connor restraining the man who helped her hold me captive. I have no chance to react before the house is filled with every cop in the Central Falls Police Department. Bennett trailing in behind them, his face filled with relief and guilt when our eyes meet.

"Ry!" he sobs as he runs toward Grey who is still holding me.

"Not right now. She needs a fucking doctor." Grey growls, holding me tighter against his chest.

I don't respond to anyone. I close my eyes and bury my face into Grey's chest, inhaling his delicious scent of sandalwood and juniper. He carries me out the front door to the waiting ambulance. Two EMTs wheel the gurney out of the back of the rig so that Grey can lay me down instead of making us climb in.

Once they have me secured into the back of the ambulance, Jodi, the EMT who is sitting in the back with me, starts to pull the door closed when Grey yanks it back open.

"If you think you're taking her out of my sight, you've lost your goddamn mind," he snarls.

She simply nods as he climbs in, sitting next to me, pulling my hand into his. When the door is closed, Jodi calls out to the driver that we're all secure and the driver takes off.

Chapter Thirty-Three

"You two can't be here," Jodi says as I open the door to see Hadley and Kat standing in the ambulance bay when we arrive.

"If you think I've been unbearable, try keeping these two away from her." I grunt.

Jodi rolls her eyes as her counterpart, Donnie, comes around the back of the ambulance to help get Ryan out.

Jodi and Donnie guide the gurney through the entrance to a room, the three of us following close behind. Once they have Ryan transferred to the hospital bed, they leave. Donnie says goodbye while Jodi simply walks out without a word. I don't blame her. I was a bit of an ass in the ambulance.

"Grey." Ryan's voice is weak. I close the distance between us. Taking her hand in mine, I press a soft kiss against her forehead as a doctor walks in.

"Excuse me, sir. Please do not touch the patient. We will need to collect evidence," Dr. McDouche announces as soon as he enters.

"Doctor, have you ever been viciously attacked so badly that you were afraid for your life and only had one person you wanted to cling to for comfort?" Hadley speaks up from behind me. Venom laces her voice like I've never heard. Sadly, she knows first hand some of the trauma that my girl endured, hers being at that fuckwit Andy's hands.

"Um, well. No, I haven't, but there are protocols in order to preserve evidence," he stutters.

"I don't give a fuck about your protocols. If my sister needs to hold onto her man after what she's been through, you will give them a moment, understood?" she snarls.

Ryan actually chuckles at Hadley's protective response.

"It's ok, babes. I just want this over with." She sighs before reluctantly releasing my hand.

I take a step back from her throwing a glare at the doctor. He ignores the daggers I'm shooting as he approaches Ryan's bedside.

"I'm very sorry for what you've been through. Is it ok if I bring our sexual assault nurse examiner in to do a thorough exam and collect any forensic evidence left?" Dr. McDouche directs the question at Ryan.

"Yes." The agreement is barely a whisper.

"Once she comes in, I will need to have everyone leave the room during the exam. You can wait right outside," the doctor announces, leaving the room before I can argue.

"It's ok, Tarzan. Let them get this over with so you can take me home." Ry's chocolate eyes pierce my soul. The usual vibrant brown is muted and dull with sadness. "Can you two give us a minute?"

Hadley and Kat both squeeze her feet, instinctively knowing she can't handle more after what she's been through, before declaring they will wait in the hall.

"What is it, beautiful?" I ask as I return to her side, taking her hand in mine.

"Grey, I love you so fucking much. I'm so sorry I didn't say it sooner. I was so afraid of you not coming back. I knew once I said the words, even if I've felt them for years, it would kill me," she rushes out before taking a breath. She wraps her arms around my bicep, holding me as close as she can. "But, I will leave with you tomorrow if it means we can be together."

"I love you too, Kitten," I smile softly at her before a light knock interrupts any additional response I can offer. The door opens and a woman dressed in scrubs enters.

"Hi, my name is Katie, I'm the SANE." Her face softens when she sees Ryan in the bed.

Her grip on my arm tightens, something the nurse notices. "Let's get you taken care of so you can get home."

"I'll be right outside, beautiful." I keep my eyes on Ry, offering a reassuring nod. "I won't let anything else happen to you."

It's been seven fucking hours since they've let me see her. I've been pacing back and forth in the hall, anxiety rippling through my veins. The exam is taking so long I'm ready to throw my fist into the wall when Jack and Bennett walk in. Jack's face shows a rage that would frighten most people.

"Where the hell have you been?" I snarl at them both.

"I was at a goddamn crime scene," Bennett snaps out in response.

"My keys were taken from me and I couldn't get a hold of anyone to pick me up." The scent of whiskey fills the air as Jack speaks, his fury coming off of him in waves.

"I'm sorry, King. There was so much happening." Bennett tries to put his arm around Jack who pushes him away.

"In Bennett's defense, I was there. There's no way he could have left, not with the shit going on at my house." I offer a sympathetic look in his direction. "Did either of them make it?"

Before Bennett can respond, the door opens and Katie walks out, looking to me.

"You may go in." She pats me on the shoulder softly before walking away with the box of evidence in her hand.

I walk through the door first, immediately seeing Ryan's puffy, red eyes. Hadley and Kat are right on my heels, followed by Jack and Bennett.

"Hey, Kitten." I quickly close the distance between us, pressing a soft kiss on her forehead.

She doesn't speak, instead simply sliding herself to the far side of the bed . She pulls me down next to her, laying her head on my chest and wrapping her arm around my torso. The room is filled with a heartbreaking silence for several moments. I can feel Ryan's heart beating through her chest against my abdomen.

Thump. Thump. Thump.

"Ry, I'm really sorry but..." Bennett pauses looking around the room, "I have to ask you some questions."

I try to shoot up from the bed but Ryan holds me tight.

"I'm not ready to talk about it with everyone around." She squeezes me tighter still, clinging to me for dear life.

Hadley and Kat stand at once both donning a sad smile on their faces. "We love you, Ry. Call us when you're home." Kat's gentle voice washes over the room.

Jack nods at me before following the girls into the hall. I know he's not going anywhere, but he's granting her wish of privacy.

"I'll be right outside with Jack, ok?" I smile down at Ryan. No matter how much I don't want to leave her side, I know she's not ready for me to hear everything yet.

After Bennett finishes questioning her, he steps out of the room.

I quickly make my way back inside, my eyes meeting Ryan's. I search them for a moment, though I don't quite know what for. It's at this moment Dr. McDouche makes his grand reappearance, only this time to announce Ryan is being discharged.

Once Ryan is dressed, I lead her out to the parking lot where Connor dropped my car off when he was done with the police.

"Did you bring Ellie?" Ryan's question takes me by surprise.

"Of course I did." I smile down at her.

"I'm sure she's pissed she had to get on a plane again." She sighs. "Hopefully, she will forgive us when we're back at your condo, and you won't have to travel like this with her anymore."

"About that..." I pause, gripping the back of my neck and chuckling before I continue.

Chapter Thirty-Four

"What do you mean, you're staying? I thought– when we were inside I said I'd come home with you." I stumble over my words, trying to understand what he's saying.

"Yes, beautiful. You said you'd come home with me. But, my home is here, with you."

Tears prick at my eyes again for the millionth time since I was taken, this time for a much sweeter reason.

"You're staying here?" I croak, needing to hear the words.

"For as long as you'll have me, beautiful." His shy smile is one I rarely see.

I let out a sob as I wrap my arms around his torso, my heart pounding in a staccato rhythm.

"How does forever sound?" I bury my face into his chest, breathing him in.

He snakes his arms around me, allowing me to adjust to the feel of him holding me close. I stiffen briefly in the embrace, my breath stuttering through the motion.

"Ry?" He pauses waiting for me to consent to more.

"Can we go to Jack's? I don't want to be anywhere that *she's* been," I croak out the request.

Grey doesn't say anything, releasing just me enough that he can look me in the eyes. His fingers graze my cheek before he opens the door to his truck, letting me in.

My eyes jerk open, my hair and body drenched in sweat. It's been like this since we arrived at Jack's days ago. No matter how much I try to block it out, I can't get through the night without the memories of my attack replaying in my sleep. Grey has been my strength through this, but I still haven't found the courage to talk about what happened. Grey stirs on the floor next to me.

"Kitten, did you have another nightmare?" His voice is soft and smooth as velvet.

"I'm ok, go back to sleep." My voice holds no confidence in the statement.

"May I come sit with you?" Grey has been sleeping on the floor since the assault, attempting to give me some space. It's a fucking double-edged sword: I wanted nothing more than closeness when he found me, but now, the idea of being touched in any capacity makes me go into an uncontrollable panic attack.

"Yea" I whisper into the darkness surrounding us.

He stands from his makeshift bed and sits next to me. "I love you, Ry." I can feel the pain in his words. I know he loves me and I know this is hurting him as much as it's hurting me, but I can't stop the lingering fear that this caused.

"I love you, more than anything in this world," I breathe as Ellie jumps on the comforter, crawling her way over to us and rolling on her back so that she gets belly rubs. Apart from Ellie, I haven't touched another living being since the hospital. She's purring between us as I give her what she came for. Grey stiffens next to me.

"Will you try something with me?" He sounds so full of hope it nearly breaks me.

I hesitate for a brief moment before replying, "Yes."

"Keep giving her rubs, I'm going to put my hand on her too, I won't move. I won't touch you. You control what happens," he explains, his idea bringing a light back into my own soul that lost hope the day I woke up chained in that basement.

I continue giving Ellie the affection she came to us for as he slides his hand into her fur as well. I don't feel him at first, but when my skin brushes his, a mixture of comfort and fear flashes through me. The memories of what she did to me and the passion that Grey and I have shared both overwhelm me. I jerk back, my eyes welling with unshed tears.

"It's ok, beautiful. It was worth a try." His voice trembles with the pain I know I'm causing him.

"I'm so sorry. I'm so, so sorry," I sob as I run out of the room.

I end up outside on the front porch, noticing Benny sitting on one of the chairs Jack put out here to people watch. He's such an old man.

"Ry?" He doesn't ask anything else, just motions to the seat next to him in invitation. I sit down, my hands covering my face as the tears fall.

"When will this be over? I'm going to lose him when I just got him! All because I can't bear to be touched," I sob into the night sky.

"Sweetheart. It hasn't even been a week." He pauses for a few moments. "Have you thought about what Hadley gave you?"

"I don't want to do it. I know I need to. I know it will help but it's going to bring up so many memories. Not only from the assault but from Mom. I don't think I can relive everything all at once." The tears continue as I explain my concerns.

"Oh, Ry. You are stronger than you're giving yourself credit. You've told me so many times how much it has helped Hadley." He worries his lip trying to find his next words. "It may be for different reasons, but you didn't cause this. You're still trying to survive it."

I stare into the night for what could be moments or hours before I respond.

"I'll make the call tomorrow." I sigh, not sure if I'm telling him or the universe at large so that it's out there. Before Benny and I can talk anymore, I hear the front door open behind me. Grey comes walking out, his beautiful chest on display sending heat to my core.

Well, at least that part of me isn't broken.

"Kitten?" he calls for me, the pet name that makes my insides melt. "Come back to bed. You need more than a couple of hours of sleep."

I stand, smiling at Benny before turning to go inside. Grey doesn't touch me as I walk by, holding the door open and staying at least a few feet away from me until I'm back in bed. He lays down on the floor next to it once more.

Chapter Thirty-Five

It's been a week today and she was gone when I woke up this morning. If I hadn't found a note on her pillow, I would be tearing the world apart. As it is, my heart nearly exploded from my chest when I woke up to an empty bed.

Be safe. Call if you need me. I love you.

Benny is with me. I'm fine. I love you, too.

While I find comfort in the fact that she's with a police officer, it's not the same as me being with her.

I walk down the stairs to see Jack lounging on the couch with a book in hand. He glances up when he sees me, once, twice, before he clears his throat.

"You look like shit, man," he chuckles. "Get dressed. Hadley asked us to come over while Ryan is out."

"If you think I'm stepping foot out of this house without coffee, you've lost your goddamn mind," I grumble under my breath.

"If you go get dressed now, I'll buy you Mud House." His voice carries through the house like music to my ears.

"Fine, I'm going," I yell back at him.

I'm still half asleep as I climb the stairs back to our room. I eventually manage to get dressed in a pair of dark wash jeans, a dark gray t-shirt and Tims. I drag my fingers through my hair while scratching Ellie behind the ear before I walk out and head back downstairs. We manage to get through the drive-thru at Mud House in record time considering how packed it is. The line is wrapped around the building and out of the parking lot onto the street.

After a fairly short drive, we arrive at Connor and Hadley's estate. *My Hellion has a damn estate, who would have thought?* I chuckle to myself, my mind stuck on how so many things have changed since I left Central Falls. Once we're granted entrance to the property, Jack pulls up to the front door. I barely open my door when Hadley comes out with Connor right on her heels. My mind instantly drifts to Ryan and how much I wish I could be that close to her right now. My guilt consumes me just as quickly, knowing she has so much trauma she needs to work through. Sighing, I exit the car, closing the door behind me and moving towards the front entrance.

"What's going on?" I look between the two of them, concern etched across my face at the pain on Hadley's.

"She's fine. We just wanted to see you, to see how you were." Nodding her head toward the door, she steps inside, the three of us following behind her. I look around, taking in the immense house surrounding us.

"Jesus, Hellion." I couldn't mask the shock in my voice even if I tried. "This isn't anything like where we grew up."

Connor outright laughs at my remark.

"I'm still not used to it." She shakes her head, "But that's not why I wanted you to come over." She continues walking, leading us through their home.

"I know my trauma may be different than what Ryan has gone through, but I have worked really fucking hard to get through it as well as I have. I may still have moments but they're less than a fraction of what they once were." She sighs, gripping Connor's hand in hers. "The reason I wanted you here is because it didn't just affect me. My actions in the aftermath affected him." Her eyes drift to Connor and back to me and I realize that she wants me to talk to him.

I collapse on the couch she's led us to.

"I love you, Greyson. If Connor didn't have his sister to talk to, I know it would have been even harder on us in the end. Please, talk to him. For her." Hadley's pleas invoking Ryan's well-being are the only thing to trigger my compliance and she knows it.

Hadley leaves Jack and I with Connor.

He's a man of few words. Stepping in front of a bar cart, he busies himself with the crystal decanter as he looks out a large floor to ceiling window. He turns back to us with three drinks, dispersing them between us.

"How are you handling things?" Connor's question takes me off guard.

I haven't thought about myself in all of this. My only concern has been Ryan.

"Honestly," I pause, gathering my thoughts. "I want to find out where they have the two motherfuckers and empty a magazine in both of them," I snarl.

"So, he's doing well." Jack snorts.

I glare at his joke. He's always been one to deflect with humor.

"My feelings don't matter, Con. She is the only one that matters in this situation. I'm not the one who was attacked," I groan, tossing my head against the back of the sofa.

"You may not have been attacked but I know from first hand experience, the love of your life pushing you away isn't something that you can get through on your own." He's calm in his response.

"I'm mad. I'm hurt. I just want to help her feel better and I don't know how. I want her to feel safe with me again." I stare at the ceiling as the words pass my lips.

"She does feel safe with you," Jack interrupts. "You're the *only* person she feels safe with. Haven't you noticed that she won't stay in a closed space with anyone else but you?"

I think back over the past week since we found her in the basement of my childhood home. Apart from the hospital, when she had to be and then to discuss the details with Benny, she hasn't been alone with anyone else. My heart rips in half at the realization. *I just want her to feel safe.*

"I'm so in love with her, but I don't know what to do. This isn't how our story is supposed to go. No one should have to go through this." I choke on the words.

"Your love for my sister has never been in question," Jack's voice cuts through my racing thoughts.

I raise a brow at him.

"OK, maybe there was a little bit of a question in the beginning." He throws a punch, jabbing me in the bicep.

Chapter Thirty-Six

I don't know why I'm not saying anything. It's not like I've never met the woman before. She was there for Hadley after everything happened with Andy. She joined us at the house when we went to help Hadley take that step in moving on. So why am I sitting here, staring past her through the open window?

"I'd say you are uncharacteristically quiet, but I get it." Amy's voice is soft and soothing. Not the feisty woman Hadley described to us when she talks about her sessions.

I still don't speak. I can't find the words. I may have agreed to this, but where do I even start?

"Have you spoken to anyone about what happened, apart from Bennett?" The question is only one of a million I've been dreading.

I shake my head.

"How have you been coping since the assault happened?" Her eyes narrow at me, not accepting my lack of communication.

I don't say anything for awhile, hoping she'll move onto something else, but she's persistent in how she watches me with that narrowed gaze. She won't let me out of this conversation. It's why I'm here after all. It's why Hadley and Benny pushed for me to make the call. To begin the journey of processing my trauma and healing.

"I haven't," I huff out a laugh. "I don't even know how to. The only person I want near me is Grey and I'm terrified to allow him to touch me because of how he might react when he finds out what they did." I trail off. Thoughts of Grey flash through my mind, breaking my heart all over again.

"You don't have to tell anyone everything right away. But," she pauses briefly. "Shutting people out will only hinder your healing process."

"How can I stop him from looking at me like a victim? Or like I'm trash?" I say my worst fears aloud, choking on the sobs that force their way out.

"You can't control anyone's reactions but your own." Her words are direct and to the point. "You can only control how you react to someone else's reaction."

I don't say anything for a moment in an attempt to process my thoughts and choose my words.

"I didn't recognize her at first. I recognized the eyes but her hair was different and her skin tone was off." I whisper.

I take a deep breath still staring past Amy, unable to look her in the eyes, to see the way she'll judge me. To see how everyone will eventually judge me when they find out.

"I didn't realize who she was until after the first time she..." My voice cracks, incapable of going on. I look down at my hands laying in my lap. Hot tears stream down my face as I relive the nightmares that plague me. "I feel guilty."

"Why do you feel guilty?" Amy's voice is a calming force, coaxing me to continue.

"Because she made me orgasm. So many times." I clutch my chest as the pain in my heart intensifies at the admission. "I didn't want to. I threw up every time, I've never felt so disgusting." The tears are coming more freely now, rolling down my cheeks before dripping off my jaw.

Amy leans forward, handing me a tissue.

"Why do you feel that it's your fault that you climaxed?" Her question seems clinical.

What the fuck kind of question is that.

"Because my body responded to her," I pause, staring at Amy like she's lost her mind.

"Your body's reaction to the stimulation was natural. Orgasms are generally involuntary. It's incredibly rare that someone can command their body to climax." She watches me, waiting for it to sink in. "You did nothing wrong. If anything, your body's reaction may have saved you."

"It may have saved me?" I ask dumbfounded.

"Sometimes in situations like you experienced, the assailant can become more violent if they don't get what they want in the moment." She keeps her tone calm even though I can see the pain in her eyes, knowing what could have been.

My first session with Amy has been on my mind all day. I didn't acknowledge where I was or what I was doing when I got home and saw Grey. I couldn't. I'm not ready to go into detail with him yet.

Today may have held some breakthroughs that I wasn't prepared for, but it doesn't mean my body will allow me to move on.

I lay in bed, my eyes glued to the ceiling. Grey is breathing steadily next to my bed as he sleeps on the floor. Ellie's laying on my chest purring like a motorboat, content as can be while I run my fingers through her long fur.

"I miss him," I whisper to her.

She mewls at me, pressing her head into my hand as I continue petting her.

"I miss how we were, how I was." My eyes begin to well with tears again. I roll onto my side, facing Grey. Ellie crawls to the opposite side, letting out an exasperated sigh as she lets her annoyance with my movement be known.

I look over the side of the bed, watching Grey like the creeper I have become. I close my eyes, willing myself to find the courage. With a deep breath I slowly drop my arm over the edge, letting it hang there like a limp extension of myself for a few moments until I summon up the determination to raise my hand mere inches from his face and softly graze his cheek with the back of my hand. His warmth sends an electric jolt through me.

Fuck, I miss him so much. I close my eyes, my arm still hanging off the side of the bed. Memories of the past few weeks and months before I was taken play through my mind. The love this man has for me is unlike anything I've ever experienced. Why am I so afraid? I open my eyes again and feeling braver yet, I run my fingers through his hair. I love his hair. It's the perfect extension of him.

With a heavy heart, I close my eyes. Even with the thoughts of the day's events racing through my mind and the realizations that I came to during my session, I find it difficult to sleep without him. Eventually, my body wins, and I fall into a deep slumber.

Chapter Thirty-Seven

I groan as the sun beams through the window above my makeshift bed waking me like the evil bastard that it is. I look at my watch and realize it's already nine a.m. I begin to roll onto my back when I realize something is in my hair.

What the fuck?

I gingerly glide my fingers through my hair only to feel more fingers. I stiffen at the discovery, continuing to roll slower than a tortoise trudging uphill through molasses in January. My heart stutters in my chest when I see my girl fast asleep with her arm dangling over the edge of the bed holding my hair like a tether to keep me near.

I relish in the feel of her hands on me, even if it's just my hair. I smile up at her face which is half hidden by the mattress. It looks like she was hanging off the bed entirely at one point while I slept. Like the selfish bastard I am, I place the hand I ran through my hair on top of hers, closing my eyes to savor the moment. My heart beats harshly in my chest as I hold her as close as she's allowed me to in the past week.

She begins to stir after a few moments, and a sharp intake of breath tells me she's awake. I don't move, worried that any movement will frighten her more. She gently tugs her hand free from under mine. I hear Ellie mewling from above me and Ryan's soft giggle makes my heart swell.

"Good morning, El."

"I've never been called that before." I can't help but chuckle at my stupid joke.

"Jesus, Grey. You scared the shit out of me," Ryan shrieks.

"Good morning, Kitten." I open my eyes, taking in the sight before me. Ryan is still laying on the bed with my traitorous cat wrapped in her arms.

Ryan's smile warms my heart.

"Did you sleep ok?" I ask, hoping she'll bring up the fact that she was touching me.

"I slept better than I have been." She sighs, not making eye contact with me. "I'm sorry if I pulled your hair while I was asleep."

I chuckle, sitting up and kneeling in front of the bed before her. "Baby, if your hands are on me, I don't care what you do to me." With a wink, I climb to my feet and walk to the bathroom.

It's the first day I've been able to come to the studio since being back. Ryan insisted on staying home, not prepared to handle being around too many people at once. Having told Nat at least about the abduction, he has been fucking amazing in helping to keep shit running even though he's trying to retire. The rest is Ryan's story to tell.

There are two other artists who have been here with Nat. One is nearing the age of retirement as well, the other closer to my age.

Shaun, the older artist, his deep olive skin weathered by years in the sun, steps out from his room with a client on his heels. They approach the front counter to take payment while I observe. The younger artist, Dixie, sits cross-legged on the couch drawing on her tablet, her kaleidoscope of long rainbow hair hanging around her. She is constantly asking how she can improve and practices tirelessly whenever I see her here. After Shaun explains the after care to his client, I ask that we all chat.

"I know you both love Nat, I do too. He was my first mentor, and he is always welcome to tattoo here whenever he chooses." I grin at Nat who shakes his head at my statement.

"You already bought the shop, son. You don't need to brown-nose me."

"What's your point, kid?" Shaun's annoyance is plain as day.

"My point is, Shaun." I level him with my gaze "While we all love him, this is my shop now and though Nat may have overlooked you selling drugs here, that is not something I'm ok with."

"He's got good weed, though," Nat snorts behind me.

"I don't give a shit what he has. It's not going to be sold out of my studio. It's my reputation on the line now. So, Shaun. Pack your shit," I say flatly.

Dixie giggles from her place on the couch. "It's about time someone called his ass out. Sorry, not sorry."

I smirk at her. She reminds me of Loki, it's going to be nice having some camaradaerie here like I did in Miami. Shaun storms out of his room with a small bag with what I assume are the drugs he's been selling from the studio.

"I'll be back for my shit when I get my truck," he growls.

"You can come by on Monday when we're closed," I call after him, knowing I'll have Bennett here with me. It's older artists like this shit who give us a bad fucking name.

Dixie looks between Nat and I before standing to her feet.

"Uh, I'm gonna go hang out in my room. Just let me know when it's safe."

She disappears behind the curtain of her workroom.

"You've known, and you haven't done shit about this? Weed I'm less concerned about; I'll blaze along with the best of them, but you don't sell the shit here, old man," I scold Nat like he's a child. He may as well be with how fucking stupid he was with this. "The asshole is selling fentanyl."

"It's not like he's going to stop. He'll just start working out of his house like we used to." His tone is cold, and he's obviously upset with me for getting rid of the artist he opened the shop with. Others have come and gone but Shaun has been here with him through it all.

"He can do whatever he wants as long as it's not here. I can't fucking believe you allowed him to do it for this long. You're fucking lucky no one caught onto it. I was here for what? Two weeks, and I realized what was going on." I shake my head. "Let's go over the shit you've left me with and figure out what I need to do from here."

I take a seat at the desk behind the counter, attempting to turn on the computer only to find that it's unresponsive.

"Tell me this thing works?" I ask, afraid I already know the answer. It looks ancient.

"Sorry, son. Never thought to replace it since I keep track of everything on paper." He winks at me before he walks out the front door.

"Son of a bitch!" I yell.

"You alright, boss?" Dixie walks up leaning against the counter.

"I will be when I find out just how fucked I am with this shop," I groan.

I spend the next several hours going through every piece of paper I can find in the shop. There is barely anything written in the ledger I found for the past month for Shaun and I know damn well he's had people in and out of that room for more than just a quick fix.

"How many people have you inked in the past month?" I ask as I look over her lines in the ledger.

"Twelve," she says shyly. "I've been trying to get my name out there more." She sounds panicked as she answers.

"Breathe. I'm just trying to see how badly I'm fucked." I go line by line and see her numbers match. "Did you fill this out for your clients or did Nat?" I raise a brow, the handwriting looks very feminine.

"I did it, Nat didn't take care of the books at all. I think Shaun had at least twenty people in the chair this month but I'd be shocked if he wrote anything up." She rolls her eyes. "Nat would let him get away with murder."

I snort at the remark.

Chapter Thirty-Eight

It's been almost two weeks since Grey carried me out of that base-ment.

"I miss him. I know he's right there; he's not going anywhere. But I miss him all the same," I admit to Amy who is sitting across from me in a large chair with her legs crossed under her.

"Have you shared any details with him yet?" The way she gets down to the point is something I will never tire of.

"I know he's not leaving me, but what if it's too much for him?" I stare down as I wring my hands in my lap.

"Have you shared any details with your friends?" she challenges. She already knows how close Hadley, Kat and I are from Hadley's sessions and from the visit we had at Hadley's old house.

"They know that it was a client. I mean they all know it was a client, that's how Grey found me." I sigh.

"How about a compromise to get your feet wet, so to speak?" She raises a brow at me. "Tell them something. Anything that you want to eventually tell Greyson."

"I'll try." I sigh

I leave our session determined to make some sort of progress. Knowing if I don't share with someone soon I'm going to become a shell of the person I once was and I refuse to let them win. I refuse to not survive this. Reaching for the pocket on my leg, I slide my phone out and unlock it, looking for the group chat.

Ryan

Can we meet somewhere? I'm not sure if Mud House is the right place but I need to talk to you both.

Pickle

Hadley and Connor's? I've been dying to sit around the fire pit.

Hadley

I'm home, come on over. Do we want drinks?

A smile pulls at my lips as I type out the words.

A bottle of wine, but what will you two have?

I pull up to Hadley and Connor's place and grin when I see Pickle and Hadley waiting for me on the front steps. Stepping out of the car, I face them, thankful that they're still willing to drop everything for me even though I haven't been up for anything since I got home.

"Hi," is all I manage before the tears start streaming down my face.

"Baby girl, it's ok. We're here." I hear Pickle's voice growing near and I freeze. "I'm not going to touch you. It's ok." Her voice is so gentle it nearly breaks me.

"Let's go into the back yard. I decided to be fancy and threw together a charcuterie board." Hadley sounds giddy.

I laugh through the tears and step toward the house.

Once we are seated in the backyard around a fire pit that Hadley had way too much fun lighting, I take a sip of my wine and look between my two friends.

"I haven't been able to talk to Grey about this." I take a deep breath before continuing, "Amy suggested I talk to you two first to break the ice."

"You can talk to us about anything." Pickle's genuine smile warms my heart.

Hadley nods next to her in agreement.

"I don't know how much I'll be able to share at once, but I'll start from the beginning." I bring the glass of wine to my lips and take a long pull.

"I didn't recognize her when she came to my car window. I thought I was just in the way of the road. I didn't realize I was being targeted." I spend the next hour going over as many details of the events that happened to me that I can handle.

Once I've finished what I can stand to share, I look up at them realizing I haven't made eye contact during the entire time I've been speaking.

"I'm proud of you." Hadley smiles at me, her face streaked with tears.

"I love you, Ry." Pickle's voice cuts through my inner thoughts.

"I love you both," I say on an exhale.

We sit in silence for a while before Connor comes out to check on us. I raise my brow at him in question.

"OK, yes. He texted me. He thought you were going to the studio after you left therapy and your phone pinged you here." Connor shakes his head. "You scared the shite out of him, kid."

I nod, knowing that Grey is probably panicking. I stand and say my goodbyes before excusing myself and racing out the front door to my car. I pull out my phone before I start the engine.

Ryan

I'm sorry, Amy had me do homework. If I didn't do it right away, I would have chickened out. I'm heading your way now.

Before he has time to respond I send another message.

Ryan

I love you, Grey.

The drive to the shop doesn't take long at all with traffic being light. When I park in front, Grey steps out to greet me before I even open the car door. I giggle, shaking my head as I exit the car.

"Kitten," he greets me with the pet name. He takes a step forward, pausing to avoid startling me. I step closer to him, closer than I have since he brought me home. I inhale his scent, but as much as I want to feel his warmth on me, I can't.

"I'm sorry, I needed to do it before I lost my nerve." I pause looking up at him from under my dark lashes. "Can we talk when we get home?"

"Whatever you need, beautiful. You don't need to be sorry, as long as you're ok." His lips turn down.

"I can't tell you everything yet, but I want to try." I gingerly raise my hand to his chest, placing just my fingertips against him. His breath hitches as I continue. "I want to be ok, I need us to be ok."

"Baby, we're ok. We'll get through anything." His breathing is still ragged, "I really want to kiss you, so before I move too quickly, I'm gonna go back inside. Come on."

I pause for a moment to watch him. I whimper softly to myself, enjoying the sight of him.

Fuck me, I need to figure my shit out.

Chapter Thirty-Nine

I've been sitting at the foot of the bed in our room for the last hour. Ryan is sitting against the headboard staring past me into space. I know she's having a hard time finding her words. When Connor texted me back saying that she was talking to the girls, I was both relieved and disappointed. I want her to feel comfortable talking to me about what's happening in that beautiful brain of hers.

"You don't need to do this now, Ry. You can tell me when you're ready." I break the silence. "I don't want you to feel pressured into telling me anything if you're not ready."

Her eyes snap to mine and she takes a deep breath before speaking. The words pour from her mouth as she tells me what happened, from the time she was kidnapped until the first time she came to. She's sobbing and shaking as she explains the initial assault. It breaks my heart, but I worry if I interrupt and remind her she doesn't need to tell me anything she's not ready to, she'll shut down entirely.

Rage courses through my body as she relives what that motherfucking psycho did to her. A fucking knife handle? She's a monster.

I keep my eyes on Ryan as she continues speaking, as if the floodgates have opened and there is no going back. When she finally stops talking she looks up at me through the tears still streaming down her face.

"I'm so sorry. I didn't mean for it to happen. I didn't want it to," she sobs.

I stand, taking a step toward where she is seated on the bed and kneel before her, making sure she is seeing my face without touching her.

"Baby, you are not at fault here, for any of it. You survived. You came home to me." I urge her to hear my words, "That is all that matters."

An hour later, Ryan lost her fight against the exhaustion from the day's events, finally falling asleep snuggled with Ellie on our bed. I leave our room and go down the stairs to find Bennett and Jack cuddling on the couch watching a movie. I step around into their line of sight before speaking.

"Every time I've brought it up, you've changed the subject." I attempt to remain calm. "Are they alive?"

Bennett doesn't speak for a long moment. I can see the wheels turning in his head as he tries to choose his words.

"Technically, yes." His response is clipped.

"What the fuck is that supposed to mean?" I snarl, the mask falling.

"She lost a lot of blood and is in a coma. He's being held without bail."

The news I was terrified to hear is almost comical.

"How long is he looking at?" I raise a brow at him.

"Theoretically, up to twenty years." His voice is low, and I know he's hiding something.

Before I can respond again, I hear Ryan scream. Dashing across the room, I take the stairs two at a time, racing to reach her. I open the door to find her sitting up in bed, her eyes closed while Ellie cowers on the edge of the bed.

"Kitten, it's OK, I'm here." I kneel down in front of her like I did earlier. "I'm right here, Kitten," I repeat my words in an attempt to pull her from the nightmare.

It takes several attempts before she comes to, looking around the room like she doesn't know what's happening or where she is. Her eyes are full of confusion and then a flash of shame takes hold.

"I'm so sorry I woke you." She sobs softly, her eyes locked on mine.

"You didn't wake me. I was downstairs." I attempt to reassure her.

"Oh," is all she says before lying down again and scooting to the other side of the bed. "Will you sit with me? At least until I fall back asleep?"

I smile at her and nod, standing up next to the bed just to take a seat on the mattress next to her.

I keep my eyes on her, humming the song *The Hell I Overcame* by Bad Omens while she relaxes back into the mattress. It takes another twenty-five minutes for her to fall back into unconsciousness, but this time I stay in the room, transplanting myself down onto my makeshift bed on the floor. I find myself staring at the ceiling for what could be minutes or hours before I fade into the darkness as well.

Flashes of her perfect ass sliding back on my thick cock as my hands are gripping her hips so tightly she'll have bruises in the morning. I groan as she slows down, tightening her pussy around me, torturing me as I allow her to have control.

"Baby, I need you to keep moving." I rasp as I dig my fingers into her flesh even more.

My eyes open to a wild mane of blonde hair spread across the pillow in front of my face. My arm wrapped tightly around her torso, snaking up her chest where my hand is cupping her breast. I freeze, my dick already hard as steel at the close proximity.

Am I still dreaming? I have to be dreaming.

I can't just move, she'll panic if I wake her. Fuck, I'm gonna get hit in the balls no matter how this goes.

I take a deep breath before I speak, smelling the mix of kiwi and mango making me forget what I was doing for a moment.

"Kitten," I whisper into her hair. "Ry, wake up."

She moans in her sleep and wiggles back against my cock.

Fuck me.

"Baby, I need you to wake up." My voice cracks.

"I don't want to. I'm comfy." She pouts into the pillow.

"I am too, but I don't want to scare you if I move." I admit quietly as I breathe her in.

She stirs next to me, grinding against me again. I try and fail to stifle the groan. A man is only so strong when the woman he loves is pressing against him like this.

I can tell when she comes to; her body goes rigid. I brace myself for impact but she relaxes back into me.

"I'm going to move away now. Ok?" I ask her, trying so hard to behave.

"It's OK. Just hold me while we sleep." She's so quiet I think I imagine the words.

"I'm gonna need to hear that again, beautiful." I hold my breath, waiting for my hopes to be shattered.

"Hold me, please?" she pleads next to me.

"Absofuckinglutely, Kitten." I smile into her hair and pull her closer.

Her steady breaths lulls me under alongside her.

Chapter Forty

I t's been a few days since I opened up and spilled my guts to Grey. Once I started, the words wouldn't stop coming out. I knew if I stopped, I would never find the courage to start talking to him about it again. We've both been sleeping better now that I can handle some closeness. The mornings are the worst for both of us. I can always feel his length when I first wake up and need pools in my core that I'm just not ready to address.

I've been spending most of my days at the shop with Grey--photographing Dixie as she tattoos clients and filming videos for the shop's social media--while he works on the business side of things. Now that Grey has made it his own, he's trying to bring everything into the digital age. With a name like Inkognito, it's too easy to play into that to get new clients' attention.

Grey smiles at me from the desk. It doesn't quite meet his eyes though. I walk over and lean against the counter looking down at him.

"What is it?" I look down at him, concern etched across my face.

"Nat hasn't been answering my calls. While I may have made certain that I only purchased the physical building and not the business itself, I'd still like to have an idea of what the numbers looked like since I took on his artists." He pauses. "Artist," he corrects.

"Have you ever heard back from Shaun on when he was getting his stuff?" I ask at the mention of only having one artist.

"Nope, my calls go to voicemail for him too." He shrugs. "Benny is aware, if I have to I'll pack up his stuff and drop it off on his doorstep."

"What do you think of me reaching out to artists on behalf of the studio to take guest spots like you did to get more people to come in who may have avoided it before?" I ask, the wheels turning in my head.

"Kitten, you are my social media manager until you tell me otherwise. If you want to reach out to artists, go for it." He grins up at me, allowing a beat to pass. "As long as you understand, no one is marking your skin but me."

I giggle as I turn away, finding my spot back on the couch. Opening my laptop, I pull up Instagram and begin searching for tattoo artists. I come across a person who seems to have a fairly large following, over fifty thousand followers, and as I scroll through picture after picture, I note the breathtaking art they've created on so many bodies.

I slide into their DMs like I have every reason to be there.

@Inkognito

Hi, I'm reaching out on behalf of the owner of Inkognito, Greyson Mancini. We were wondering if you would be interested in doing a guest spot for a couple of weeks out of our studio.

@LowkeyInkz

Are you kidding me? Fuck yes! Do you have room for three artists?

I pause for a moment, confused they want to bring more artists? I walk over to the desk and peer down at Grey.

"Yes, Kitten?" he asks as soon as he feels my eyes on him.

"Could you house three guest artists at once?"

"What? You have three people wanting to take guest spots at once?" His question is full of confusion.

"What can I say, my man's name holds weight." I giggle.

"I love you," he chuckles, shaking his head. "Yes, we'll make it work."

@Inkognito

Sure, how do the last two weeks of August sound?

Knowing that is only a couple of weeks away, I suck in a breath waiting for a response.

@LowkeyInkz

We'll be there. Tell the boss man we'll see him soon. (wink emoji)

Boss man?

I open up the artist's page again and look at the name, it doesn't ring a bell but as I scroll further back into the pictures I notice a picture of Jack watching the Great British Baking Show with a man I don't know on a familiar looking couch.

"Uh, Grey, what are the names of the artists at Urban?" I call over to him from my spot on the couch.

He looks up at me, his brow furrowed in confusion. He tells me their names and I start giggling, unable to control myself.

"Kitten?" The question barely passes his lips when the front door of the studio swings open.

A woman who looks strangely familiar walks in.

"Anya?" Grey smiles at her like they're old friends.

"Hey! I didn't expect to see you here." She flashes a bright smile at him. "How did everything turn out with," she doesn't finish when she sees me sitting on the couch.

Grey grins at me, "It's great. Ryan, this is Anya. Anya, Ryan."

I stand and cross the room, taking her in.

Anya, why does that name sound familiar?

"Do I know you?" My voice comes out harsher than I intended.

"No?" She looks between Grey and I. "I have an appointment with Dixie."

"Hey, bestie! Come on back, I can't wait to work on this poly piece. It's going to be beautiful!" Dixie pops her head out from around the corner, and they walk off together.

"How do you know her?" I stare at Grey nervously. I know he has a past, but I'm used to the past that lives here. My heart begins racing in my chest like I'm being chased by Freddy Krueger. What if he slept with someone else while I've been incapable of being close?

I fight the tears trying to prick their way from my eyes.

"Baby, no. We met at a bar months ago when I first got back," His voice is calm as he rushes to me like he immediately senses where my mind has gone. "I went out with Jack. We just chatted. Nothing happened. She's involved with someone, and I want you. Only. You." He enunciates the last two words slowly.

I nod, unable to speak, my heart still mid-marathon. Grey cups my cheek with his hand, tilting my chin so that my eyes meet his.

"I am yours. I will always be yours." He wraps his free hand around my waist holding me flush against his hard body.

I close my eyes, pressing my forehead against his chest, inhaling his magnificent, masculine scent.

I really need to find a way to bottle that up.

Chapter Forty-One

R yan has allowed me to hold her while we sleep every night over the past couple of weeks. I'm so fucking thankful she's beginning to allow me to be close to her again. She's been spending every few days having sessions with Amy; the progress she's made in such a short amount of time makes me hopeful. I'm not naive enough to believe she's going to allow anything more than me holding her for the time being, but a man can hope.

She finished her antibiotics and got her most recent STD screening back yesterday. It was negative. She's been concerned because of how long some diseases can take to show as positive. I know she's been talking through her worries with Amy. I just wish I could help more.

I'm sitting on the couch at Inkognito, sketching a piece for a client who is coming in tomorrow, when the door crashes against the wall. I jump to my feet and see Ry standing there with a look of determination on her face.

"Kitten, what's wrong?" I put down my tablet and start to close the distance between us when she runs full speed at me. I pause, unsure of what's happening and not wanting to scare her. Before I have time to do anything but react, she's jumped onto me, her legs wrapped around my waist. I cup her ass with my hands, holding her up. Her fingernails dig into my scalp as she urges my face closer to hers. Her lips find mine like a beacon in the night. Ryan's moan at the connection sends all of my blood straight to my dick. I carefully back up to the couch and lower myself, sitting back while she straddles my thighs. I wrap my arms around her waist, holding her against me, allowing her to keep control of our kiss no matter how badly I want to take over. She swipes her tongue at my lips, and I open for her as she deepens the kiss. I groan into her mouth and gently pull away, panting.

"Kitten, what's going on?" I ask, still trying to catch my breath and get my dick under control before I start humping her leg like a stray dog off the street.

"I need you, Grey." She pouts as she grinds against my length.

"Fuck, baby," I grind out. "I'm taking you home."

I lower her to the floor. Her body sliding down my length does nothing but make the need to take her right here even more overwhelming. She giggles when she can see I'm struggling to restrain myself. I grab my tablet from where I dropped it and lead her outside to my truck. When she reaches the passenger door, I spin her around so she's facing me again.

Caging her against the door, I press my hips against her belly so she can feel me. I graze my fingers down her cheek before tilting her chin and crashing my lips to hers again for a brief moment. The sexiest little whimpers leave her mouth as I consume her.

"If you need me to stop, you tell me. Understand?" I stare into her eyes hoping to convey my seriousness.

"I know, I'll tell you." She smiles as she cups my cheek with her hand. I can't help but lean into her touch. "Take me home."

I may have run every red light that I came to. I have absolutely no regrets though, because the way my girl has been squirming in her seat for the last fifteen minutes has my cock harder than steel. When I park in front of Jack's house and see that his car isn't here, I breathe a sigh of relief. I exit the truck and while I'm rounding the bed, I send a quick text to Bennett.

Greyson

Please keep Jack out tonight.

Bennett

Ew, she's like my sister too, you know. But, yeah I'll get him to stay here.

I grin when I look back up to see Ryan leaning against the passenger door waiting for me.

"What were you doing?" She arches a brow at me.

"Just making sure we have the house to ourselves." I press a soft kiss against her temple and wrap my arm around her waist, leading her inside.

"You told Jack!" She slaps my chest.

"No, I told Bennett to get Jack to stay there tonight." I wink at her.

"Oh my god." She laughs at me. "I don't know if I love you more or if I'm embarrassed that they know."

"Beautiful, it's not like they don't know we've had sex." I chuckle darkly. "If you remember, I made sure they knew after they kept you up for an entire night."

"That was a fun morning." Her soft lips twitch, trying desperately not to give away her amusement.

I lead her up to our room, and once the door closes and I turn to face her, she latches herself onto me again. My back is against the door, her fingers digging into my scalp, pulling the strands in the most delicious way. She presses soft kisses against my lips and then lowers to my neck and chest. She claws at my shirt, lifting it until I raise it over my head and toss it onto the floor.

I'm not used to giving up control, but I know she needs this. She drops to her knees and hooks her fingers under the waistband of my pants tugging them over my hips and down my thighs, freeing my rock-hard cock which stands at attention waiting for instruction.

"What do you need, baby?" I ask as I run my fingers through her beautiful blond locks.

"I need —" Instead of finishing her sentence she swipes her tongue along the slit of my tip, swirling circles around the head with her warm, wet tongue before taking me into her mouth. She sucks me deep, not allowing herself anytime to adjust.

"Christ, Ry," I curse, fisting my hands at my sides, desperately trying to control myself.

She continues fucking me with her face, her nails digging into my ass as she forcefully thrusts my cock in and out of her mouth. I'm panting, bright spots clouding my vision as my release nears.

"Ry," I groan, unable to complete my thought.

With an audible pop, she releases me.

"Grey, if you don't fuck my mouth like you want to, I'm going to scream." She's panting, her voice low and husky, filled with desire, "I need this too."

She slides my cock back in her mouth and without giving her time to adjust, I tangle my fingers into her hair, thrust myself inside her perfect mouth, and groan at the sensation. I look down, our eyes meet, and she slightly nods, giving me permission. With that, any control I had left dissipates as I fuck her throat, my balls tightening with every pass over her tongue. The most beautiful tears stream down her face as I take what I need and give her what she asked for.

"Fuck, Ry" I manage through gritted teeth as my release spills down the back of her throat. Bright white spots take over my vision, leaving me unable to see for several moments. When everything comes back into focus I see Ryan still kneeling in front of me with a proud grin on her face.

Chapter Forty-Two

"Oh, Kitten." Grey's voice is soft as he takes me in, still on my knees. "I don't know what the hell I did to deserve that."

"You've just been you." I smirk up at him. He holds his hand out to help me stand, which I accept, pulling myself to my feet.

I lean against his bare chest, peppering a few soft kisses along his chiseled form. He leads me to the bed and keeps his eyes on mine as he slowly peels off the graphic t-shirt I stole from him this morning. When he sees I'm not wearing a bra his eyes light up. He leans forward, pressing a kiss to the top of each breast.

"If you close your eyes, whatever I'm doing stops. Understood?" His insistence to make sure I stay present with him warms my heart.

"Eyes on you. Got it." I wink

"Don't sass me, woman." He groans. "I want you–fuck, do I want you–but I'm not going to do anything to hurt you."

"I know you're not. If I thought you were, I wouldn't be here right now. I love you, Grey. I trust you." I place my hand on his chest, over his heart. "I love you," I repeat.

"Fuck me." He groans.

"That's the plan." I giggle. His brow arches at me in warning. I can't help when another laugh passes my lips.

He kneels down in front of me this time, hooking his fingers into the waistband of my yoga pants. He tugs the fabric down until my bare legs are exposed, my pink thong still covering my pussy. He slowly runs his fingers from my ankles to my thighs. I gasp at the feel of his hands on my skin for the first time in over a month.

"You ok?" His gaze locks on mine.

I nod my head in response.

"No, Kitten, use your words."

"Yes," I breathe.

The warmth of his skin against mine feels like heaven. His fingers ever so slowly trail to the apex of my thigh. He grazes the length of my pussy with the tips of his fingers before tapping my clit. I moan at the sensation, my eyes fluttering closed, and he stops. My eyes fly open, and I whimper.

"Eyes on me." His voice is gravelly with desire.

"Yes, Daddy." I pant. "Please, don't stop."

The devilish grin that spreads across Grey's face sends another rush of molten arousal straight to my core. His fingers continue slowly massaging the tiny bundle of nerves hidden beneath the flimsy fabric he still hasn't removed. I'm writhing beneath his touch as my climax builds. My eyes are locked on his as he continues to coax the orgasm out of me. My control falters, and I finally reach the peak, trembling in the best way under his touch as I reach the crescendo. My release rolls through me as wave after wave of bliss brings so many emotions, I'm torn between laughing and crying.

"Beautiful?" Grey's sitting on the bed with his arms wrapped around me in an instant as I come down from my high.

"I'm ok, that was perfect." I laugh, which comes closer to a sob.

"Whatever is happening right now doesn't seem like it was perfect." He sounds defeated.

"No, I promise. I'm ok." I pull back, cupping his jaw with my hands, pouring my soul into him through my eyes. "I was afraid that after she forced me to orgasm, I wouldn't be able to when I wanted and when I needed to." My thoughts are all jumbled together as I try to express myself.

Grey's face softens, and he presses his lips against mine. The kiss is so much different than the ones we shared earlier. The love and compassion consume me as he holds me close to him, my legs wrapping around his waist, connecting us as closely as I can manage. I feel his arousal at our proximity. My hips gyrate against him as he continues to grow between us.

"Baby, we don't need to do anything else," he groans into my mouth.

"I want to. I need to," I admit sheepishly.

I press on his chest so that he falls to his back on the bed.

"Take what you need. You're in control." His cocky grin has me panting with need already.

I lean over and pull a condom from the nightstand drawer. Tearing it open with my teeth, I carefully pull it out and roll it down his long, thick shaft to the base. I stand next to the bed for a moment and wiggle myself out of the lacy pink thong. Once it's discarded on the floor, I climb back onto the bed, straddling Grey's thighs. He grips my hips, which startles me slightly, and my eyes meet his.

"Are you sure?" His expression is full of concern.

"I've never been more sure about anything in my life. I need to feel you inside me." I grin at him as I lower myself onto his perfect cock.

I groan at the intrusion, it feels so good and I haven't even started moving yet. I feel so full; it's magnificent. I don't move for a moment, appreciating the sensation that having him inside me brings.

"Talk to me," The desire in his voice is potent.

I start to grind my clit against him once he's fully seated inside my tight pussy.

"Fuck, Ry." His groans at my actions are my undoing.

I slowly begin to raise myself up and down, pumping my pussy full of him. It's not the same. But even the barrier of the condom can't take away from how fucking amazing it feels.

"Grey." His name on my lips like a prayer as I continue fucking him.

I move quicker as I feel sensations building in my core, undulating my hips each time he's fully buried. The friction against the sensitive bundle of nerves sends me over the edge. I cry out again as my walls tighten around him, and his hands grip my hips as he drives himself into me, once, twice, three times before he shouts out his release. I feel him swell inside of me as he empties into the condom. I collapse onto his chest, enjoying the feel of his skin against mine once more. His arms wrap around my back, holding me tight as he slides from inside me and maneuvers me so that he can remove the condom and toss it in the bedside can before he wraps himself around me once more.

"Talk to me, Kitten," he whispers into my hair.

"I've been needing you so badly, needing this, so badly." I contemplate my next words before I continue, "She took so much from me and I have been so lost in my head thinking she would take this away from us too."

"Ryan, nothing could take me from you. I would fight like hell to get back to you." I feel him smile into my hair as he holds me tight.

Ryan has been jumping me multiple times a day since we broke the seal, so to speak. It's barely been a week but I'm dying to taste her again. I know she's not ready for that. She's been using me like her own personal fuck toy and my god am I here for it.

I've just finished with a client and walk them to the counter to take payment. I smirk when I see Ryan sitting on the couch on her phone.

She's still not ready to be on her own with photography. I know she misses it with how much she's been photographing the artists here. I'm hoping my surprise for her will help her heal in that aspect too.

"It was great working with you, Taryn." I smile at her, handing over the ointment she purchased and a sheet of aftercare instructions which I've already gone through in the workroom. I've found over the years having the printout helps. They tend to be so excited and looking at their new ink that they don't pay attention to the instructions in the room.

"Thanks so much, Greyson. I'll let you know when I'm ready for another!" She grins and waves to Ryan before leaving through the front door.

I saunter over to where Ryan is sitting and join her, pulling her feet onto my lap.

"Hey, gorgeous." I gently massage her calves, "What do you think about—" before I can ask my question we're cut off by the front door opening. I look over to see Bennett standing there, looking sheepish.

"Mind if I use your restroom? Afternoon coffee may have been a little too strong." He chuckles.

"Yeah man, that's fine." I laugh.

"Uh, Benny. I love you but spray. Your shit stinks worse than a rotten egg mixed in gasoline," Ryan calls after him which makes Bennett and I both laugh as he disappears into the back of the shop.

"So, Kitten, what do you think about —" The front door slams open again. This time, I jump to my feet and shield Ryan from a rabid-looking Shaun. He looks strung out on a bad supply of whatever he's been selling.

"Shaun, what are you doing here?" I ask as calmly as possible while keeping Ryan out of sight behind me.

"I'm here for my shit," he snarls at me.

"OK, how about you schedule a time outside of normal hours so that we don't have any clients coming in and getting in the way of your things?" I keep my voice steady, but his demeanor has me ready to step in front of a bullet for my woman.

"How about I get what I came here for now." Shaun's tone is even more erratic than when he first walked through the door.

"What is it that you want?" My calmness wavers as he steps closer to us. I can tell the moment he realizes Ryan is behind me because his lips twitch into a dark grin.

"I want the cunt that cost me the biggest payday," he growls.

"What the fuck are you talking about?" I snap at him.

"You think it was a coincidence that Ing and Trav came after her as soon as you made a move? Who the fuck do you think told her that she was going to miss out if she didn't act fast?" He snorts as though it should be obvious. "They were here the night you two fucked and made out right there in front of the window." He motions at the large window behind us.

"What exactly was in it for you?" I arch a brow as I see Bennett slowly walking toward us.

"She was a fucking cash cow. If you would have stayed out of it and let her finish doing what she wanted, she would have given me her supplier so I didn't have to go through her anymore." The more he speaks, the more I feel Ryan's rage building behind me.

I place my hand on her hip, trying to comfort her while keeping her out of his sight as best I can.

"Let's ignore the fact that she's the love of my life for a moment. You're telling me that you sold a woman to a psychopath for more drugs?" I spew the words at him like venom.

"What of it?" His demeanor changes before my eyes. He's offended that I find his actions appalling.

I'm barely holding myself back when I no longer feel Ryan under my touch. She's maneuvered herself around me and is charging toward a strung-out Shaun.

"Ry, no!" I try to pull her back into my arms, but she leaps onto the coffee table, winding her arm back and punching with more force than I realized she had, landing the most graceful right hook to his eye that I've ever witnessed. He collapses onto the ground before he can react. I wrap my arms around her stomach and pull her back to me, lifting her off of the table and walking us back to the other side of the couch while Bennett calls in for backup.

"Baby, talk to me," I urge Ryan once I get her to turn around and look me in the eyes.

"I'm fine. I'll never understand it, but I'm fine." She wraps herself around me for a brief moment before excusing herself to use the restroom.

"Backup will be here momentarily, but," he pauses glancing back where Ryan disappeared to the bathroom. "He's got no pulse."

"What?" I look between Shaun's lifeless body and Bennett.

"My guess is whatever he was on took him out either when she landed the punch or when he landed on the ground." He pauses. "Either way, he's gone. There's more though. Apparently, our friend here paid a visit to Ingrid or Luna, whatever we're calling her, about an hour before he arrived here. She was pronounced dead fifteen minutes ago."

I collapse onto the couch, unsure how to process what he just said. *How the hell is Ryan going to handle this?*

As if she's hearing my thoughts, she appears behind Bennett. Her eyes barely meet mine, but as soon as our gazes lock, she knows. She rushes toward me and bursts into tears. I pull her into my lap, holding her tight.

Chapter Forty-Four

The police and EMT finally left the shop with Shaun's body after what felt like hours. I'm relieved that it feels like it's finally over and that things make more sense, even if I still don't understand why Ingrid set her sights on me to begin with. When they questioned me this time, they asked if I had any idea that Ingrid or Travis were under the influence. They didn't think it was an important factor to share prior to Shaun's appearance here today.

Grey hasn't left my side since this all went down and I couldn't be more thankful to have this amazing man by my side.

"Kitten." He pauses, dropping my hand to walk to the door and lock it now that we're alone. Once he returns to the couch, he sits down next to me. Pulling my legs into his lap, he begins absentmindedly massaging my calves, instantly melting away the stress of the day.

"Grey," I say his name, teasingly. I stare at his face for some sort of clue as to what's coming.

"Kitten," he repeats, his expression giving nothing away. "How would you feel about opening a studio attached to the shop here?"

"I mean, I would love it, but how would we even manage that?" I ask, looking around the space.

"Jack has plans drawn up that he will go over with you. But if you want it, I will make it happen." He grins at me. "Selfishly, I don't want to be far from you."

"Oh my god," I shriek and wrap myself around him.

I have been wanting so badly to get back into photography, to be behind a lens again. I'm not sure if I want to continue doing boudoir, but I need to be back behind the camera in a more constant capacity. As much as I enjoy helping Grey with his social media, I need to do something more with my passion.

Our tongues tangle together as I grind against his length, ready to thank him with my body for this gesture, when a loud knock sounds on the front door.

With all of the commotion this afternoon, I completely forgot about his surprise.

"Oh my god," I squeal, jumping to my feet and scrambling to the door.

Grey groans on the couch, adjusting himself.

"Hi! Come on in, he's right over there." I grin at the three guests and motion for them to walk into where Grey is sitting.

"What the fuck are you doing here?" Grey's smile is brighter than I've seen outside of the bedroom in awhile.

"Surprise, bossman!" Loki giggles as they wrap their arms around his neck.

I stand back, watching the reunion. Niall and C both bring him in for an awkward man hug. You know, the one where they barely clap each other's shoulder.

"This is why you asked who worked at Urban a few weeks ago?" Grey shoots me a wicked grin and I nod shyly at him.

With as much as I went through, he never faltered in his support and stayed by my side the entire time. He needs this reunion and the family he found in Miami as much as I need him here.

Hadley, Kat, and I sit around a table inside Mud House sipping our heavenly bean juice when Kayleigh struts over and takes up the fourth seat, joining us.

"This is the first time I think you've ever stopped working while we've been here," Hadley teases.

"What can I say? I needed some girl time. They've got it under control today." Her warm smile brightens the room.

"So, what's new?" Kat asks, looking around at each of us expectantly.

"Grey and Jack are working out how to build a studio for me that's somehow connected to the tattoo shop. Our next step is finding a place so we can move out of Jack's." I smirk at them. "Now that we're going at it like rabbits once again, it's safer for everyone involved if my brother isn't within earshot."

Hadley and Kat start giggling at that while I take a long swig of my coffee.

"Joel can help you find a place if you'd like." Kayleigh smiles, placing her hand on mine.

"That would be amazing! I don't even know what we want or need," I sigh.

"Don't worry, he's great at that. He tolerated not only house hunting with me after the divorce but also when we found each of the Mud House locations." She laughs aloud at the memory.

Kayleigh picks up her phone, tapping on the screen for a moment before putting it back down.

"He'll text you soon." She grins.

The four of us chat for quite a while, Hadley sharing her concern about Connor acting strange. My best friend has been through a shit show in the past year and a half too, so I know she's struggling. We do our best to reassure her that everything is fine. I remind her to talk to Amy. I will forever credit that woman for how she's helped me so much.

"Amy has been helpful for Liam and me too. Immediately after my abduction, Liam had a hell of a time processing his guilt. Amy was phenomenal in helping us through that." Kayleigh's admission takes me off guard. "Plus, she was integral in Joel and I being able to get to where we are now."

"Amy has treated all of us?" I arch a brow and snort. "We are quite the friend group, aren't we?"

"Cheers to trauma." Hadley raises her mug. We all laugh and click our mugs together.

Kayleigh eventually ends up returning to the counter, finishing her work day. Hadley leaves to meet Connor for some corporate event, which leaves Kat and I alone.

"If he doesn't do it soon, she's going to have an aneurysm," Kat snorts.

"I know, she looks like she's about to burst from the anxiety. I'll text him." I shake my head.

[text message]

Ryan

Time is running out, dude. She's spiraling.

Several minutes go by with no response, but I can see he's read the message. I smile, knowing he's probably with her and he's already been panicking himself.

When my phone does go off, it's from a number I don't have saved. I'm relieved to see it's Joel; he has availability this afternoon.

Chapter Forty-Five

I'm sitting behind the counter at Inkognito, and it's like old times with Loki, C, and Niall. They're chatting away with Dixie, who is animated and excitedly accepting critiques from the seasoned artists. I grin at the sight. Fuck, I've missed them.

My phone lights up with a text, and my grin widens when I see the name, grabbing the device off of the desk.

Ryan

Do you think you could sneak away for a few hours this afternoon?"

Greyson

For you, anything. I just need to get another box. We used the last one this morning.

I discreetly adjust myself as the morning's events run through my mind.

Ryan

I'm not against that, actually. I insist on it, but not until later because Joel said he can make time for us to discuss what our wishlist is for a house.

Chuckling at myself, I type out a response.

Greyson

I'll be there. Love you, Kitten.

I knew we had people requesting appointments online for the guest spots for the past few weeks since announcing that they'd be here, but I didn't realize just how popular the idea would be. Even Dixie is booked through the next two weeks after Lo and Niall reposted some of her work on their socials. I've been reaching out to other artists I think will be interested in getting guest spots scheduled for every month.

Looking at the time, I realize I've got to head out. I walk back to where Dixie is working and knock on the doorframe. She's got the curtain open while she works on a woman's thigh.

"Hey, what's up?" She grins up at me and pulls the tattoo machine away from her client's skin.

"I'm heading out to meet Ry. I'll be back later, ok?" I arch a brow at her, it's the first time she's been in *charge*.

"Yeah, we're fine. Get out of here. Tell her to come by later though. I want to talk to her about a book I got," she says as she waves me away.

I walk through the door at Mud House to see Kayleigh in an embrace with a man I've never seen before. He has hair almost as dark as the night sky and has his arms wrapped tightly around Kayleigh's body. Ryan is holding a little girl in her arms who is energetically talking about an episode of Bluey. Another man with dark hair is kneeling in front of her, next to a little boy with red hair that matches Kayleigh's.

Two things happen in quick succession. My heart swells at the thought of Ryan holding our child, and images of our entire future form in my mind. I grin at the thoughts as I approach them.

I lightly press the palm of my hand against Ryan's back when I reach her.

"Hey, beautiful," I smirk at Ryan before acknowledging the rest of the group. Kayleigh introduces the man who is holding her as her husband, Liam, and the man with her doppelganger is her ex-husband, Joel.

"Why did you draw all over your body?" The doppelganger, Brady, asks me when his dad stands to shake my hand. "Mommy won't let Daisey and I draw on our bodies."

I chuckle, "I had to wait until I was much older to start drawing on myself. Trust me, wait for it. There are some that I don't like anymore and I want to change."

"Can I change the ones you don't like?" He grins up at me like he's about to win the lottery.

"If your parents are ok with it, absolutely." I smirk at him.

"Daddy, Dad, Mommy! Can I?" He jumps up and down pulling at whatever garment he can on each of the three adults.

"Maybe later. Right now, Daddy has to talk to Ryan and Greyson about finding them a house," Liam chuckles as he takes Daisey from Ryan's arms.

"Bye, sweet girl and thank you again, Kayleigh." Ryan smiles and waves goodbye to Liam and Brady.

I walk back into the shop to find Loki and Dixie working on practice skin. Lo is teaching Dixie how they do the stippling technique, which is something Dixie has been struggling with. C and Niall are sitting on the couch watching The Great British Baking Show, of course. I can't help but roll my eyes at the memories of the two of them fighting over the TV.

"What did you have to give up to watch this time?" I ask Niall as I join them on the couch.

"Nothing, we've come to an understanding." His smile is unnerving.

"Um, should I be scared?" I arch a brow and glance between the two of them.

"Nope, I've just decided that I'd like to buy Urban Ink." His smile grows. "If the offer is still on the table."

"Absolutely, man! I'm so happy for you. I'll call my lawyer in the morning." I reach over and shake his hand.

C shakes his head in disgust.

"I can't believe I'm going to have to watch this shit," he groans.

"I listen to you and Lo fuck all the time. You can tolerate my obsession with baking." Niall snorts.

Lo walks over to us and presses a kiss to C's temple before turning on their heel. "He's right, sir. Plus, I'm a fan because it just means that you'll spend even less time in front of the tv and more time inside me."

"What the hell did I just walk in on?" Ryan's face is redder than a lobster fresh out of a steaming pot.

I snort and close the distance between us. "Something I am thankful you just interrupted, Kitten." I wrap my arms around her waist and pull her in tight to my chest. Raising my hand to caress her cheek, I grip her chin between my fingers and tilt her face for easier access to her lips. Our lips barely brush against each other when she whimpers into my mouth. Chuckling softly, I pull away from her.

"On that note, I'm out. Dixie, lock up." I stand, shaking Niall's hand again.

"Woohoo! Get it, bossman," Lo cheers behind us. I flip them off as Ry and I walk back out the front door.

"Were you and Joel able to find anything you liked?" I ask as I walk with her to my truck.

"Yea, there is one I really liked, but I want you to see it before we make an offer." I open the door for her to slide in, but before I can step back she pulls me in for another quick kiss. "Take me home."

Chapter Forty-Six

We finally get back to Jack's place, and I don't bother waiting for Grey to get my door, opening it myself and slipping out. I take a few steps, meeting him at the back of the truck.

"You're in a rush tonight." His smile is contagious.

"I'm ready to try." I smirk up at him, my heart hammering in my chest.

His eyes go wide, and without saying another word, he bends down and lifts me, tossing me over his shoulder. I start giggling and playfully slapping his ass as he races inside. The door barely closes behind us before he's taking the stairs three at a time. He tosses me down on the bed as soon as we get to our room. Ellie scrambles out the door and he closes it behind her.

"Fuck me, that was hot." I giggle.

"Later, you can't throw this out there and not let me at least try." My pussy tightens from the look of hunger in his eyes.

"Yes, Daddy," I manage to whisper.

"Good girl. Remember, eyes on me." He hooks his fingers under the waistband of my pants, dragging them down my legs.

His deep groan when he realizes I haven't been wearing panties sends heat straight to my core. My pants are thrown somewhere in the room. I toss my head back as I feel his lips trailing soft kisses up my calves to my thighs. His warm breath along the length of my pussy sends me into a frenzy.

"Grey, please," I whimper.

"Patience, Kitten." I can feel his grin against the apex of my thigh.

I feel his breath against my pussy again as he inhales my scent. I whimper and buck against him. His arms wrap around my thighs and I feel him tilt his head before he speaks.

"Eyes. On. Me," he reiterates. "You know I will stop if I see your eyes close. I need to know you're here with me, beautiful."

"Please, Grey." The plea passes my lips as he swipes his tongue up the length of my pussy until it's swirling around my clit and I moan loudly at the sensation.

My vision goes fuzzy, and I forget where I am as he sucks my clit between his lips.

"Oh fuck," I cry out. Everything becomes clear again as he slides his tongue inside me, fucking me with an intensity unmatched from any other time we've been together. I grip his hair as I feel my climax building in my core. He pulls his tongue out, sucking my clit between his lips again, then swirling his tongue so quickly around the sensitive bundle of nerves that I see stars.

"Oh, my god, Grey. Don't stop," I beg between breaths.

He pulls away long enough to ask, "Stay with me?"

His tongue is swirling in tight circles again before I can attempt to form a response when his thick fingers slide against my entrance. I stiffen briefly, going back to that basement, but he pulls my clit between his lips again, bringing my attention back to the present.

His thick digit slides inside of me as he continues to feast like I'm his last meal.

My pussy starts to convulse when another finger starts to press gently on my tight hole. As he places more pressure on my cave of wonders, my orgasm detonates, and my pussy clenches around him so tightly his hand becomes immobilized until my high subsides.

"Jesus fucking Christ, Ry," he growls as he trails kisses up my stomach, lifting the tank top I'm still wearing. "Does this shirt hold any sentimental value to you?" He raises a brow.

"What?" I look at him in confusion. My body is still humming after the explosive orgasm. "No, why?"

He grips my top in both hands at the neck and tears it from my body, exposing my breasts. His hand cups one breast while his mouth latches onto the other, swirling his tongue around the pebbled peak and pulling it between his lips. I arch my back into the sensation his attention brings.

"Grey, please." I dig my nails into his shoulders as I claw at his shirt, pulling it up his back and over his head.

"What do you need, beautiful?" His grin is wicked. He knows exactly what I want.

"Claim me." I drag him closer to me and press my lips against his, tasting myself on him. "All of me," I whimper as I feel his stiff length glide against my clit. I pull away, staring into his eyes.

"Ry," he chokes on my name as his fingers grip my hair at the base of my skull, crashing his lips against mine.

With a swipe of his tongue, I open to him. My taste on his tongue infiltrates my senses, causing me to melt even deeper into him. I wrap my arms around his neck, holding him as close as I can. He slides a hand between us, working my clit with his fingers, rubbing tight circles. I'm moaning into the kiss as he edges me closer and closer to a release before he stops, pulling away to grab a condom from the new box. Once it's on, he wastes no time, sliding inside me until he's fully seated. A string of curses passes my lips as I envelop him. I thrust my hips up to meet his, urging him to move.

His hand, which is still in my hair, tilts my head back, giving him access to my throat. He gently nibbles and sucks as he slowly slides in and out of me. I moan softly, my legs wrap around his hips, digging my heels into his ass; I need more.

"Mine." The growl comes from deep in his chest as he thrusts inside of me so hard my pussy convulses around him instantly.

"Yours, always yours," I cry out.

His hand is still working my clit as he fucks me with no restraint until I come undone. My body goes limp as the orgasm takes over. I feel him lean down, pressing a soft kiss to my neck as his lips curve into a smile.

Without warning, I'm flipped onto my stomach, I giggle in surprise at the quick movement. Grey's lips pepper kisses down my body to the small of my back. He gently massages my ass cheeks before sliding his hands back down so that his fingers find my pussy, filling me once again. It doesn't take him long before I'm cutting off the circulation to his fingers as he coaxes yet another orgasm from me. I've got no bones left in my body when I hear his voice.

"Are you sure?" The desire in his voice has me needing more already.

"Yes, for fuck sake. Daddy. Fill me. Claim me. Show me I'm yours, only yours." I whine.

The sound that leaves his throat is animalistic as he rubs circles around my tight hole with a finger while his other hand is still fucking my dripping pussy.

"Grey, I'm gonna come again." I whimper as his fingers find my g-spot. He lessens the pressure and the sensation dissipates. "Fucker."

"Oh, I'm going to." He chuckles darkly at his joke as he removes his hand from my ass for a second. When he returns, his fingers are wet with his saliva, and he slowly slides the tip of a finger in, working my asshole like he does my pussy.

My body, still limp from the multiple orgasms, is starting to become more alert. He manipulates his hand in my pussy to simultaneously reach my clit and g-spot, causing an orgasm to detonate.

"Fuck, Grey. Grey. Yes, Grey!" I chant as I fall over the cliff, the climax rolling on for several minutes.

Before I have time to come down, I feel his cock inside my pussy again as multiple fingers are in my ass. I nearly see stars, but he pulls out before I go floating into another orgasm. His fingers leave my ass, and I feel the blunt head of his cock pressing against my tight hole.

"Stay with me, Kitten," he groans as he works himself inside me.

"Oh, god, Grey," I whimper softly as he slowly seats himself inside my ass.

His hand wraps around my waist, finding my clit again as he works himself in and out until I fully relax into the experience.

"Ry?" he whispers as he bends down, biting my shoulder.

"Fuck. Me." The plea barely passes my lips as he thrusts into my ass, making sure I feel every inch of him.

"Jesus fucking Christ, Ry!" He groans so loudly when he reaches climax. He pinches my clit, my pussy and ass convulse simultaneously as I come so hard my vision goes dark apart from the white spots in my peripheral.

Chapter Forty-Seven

My heart is pounding so hard in my chest as I collapse, pulling out of her glorious ass and landing on my side on the bed. I have never felt so sated in my entire existence.

"Are you ok?" I breathe as I pull her into my arms, her back flush against my chest.

"I've never been better," she giggles as she wiggles against my cock.

"Fuck, baby." I chuckle and lightly slap her ass. "Give me a few minutes."

I press a kiss into her hair as I get up and go into the bathroom to clean up. I can't help but smile at the trust she's given me. I love her so goddamn much. I find myself wondering what would have happened if I had stayed all those years ago. Would we have ended up where we are now?

"Grey?" I hear Ry's tired voice over the running water.

"Be right there." I grab a second washcloth when I'm done cleaning myself and run it under the warm water.

I return to her and gently clean between her legs and gingerly check her ass to make sure she's ok. I toss the damp rag into the tub and get back into bed. I pull her close to me again and her steady breathing lulls me to sleep with her.

I wake to a very angry Ellie jumping on my chest and practicing her southpaw moves to my jaw. She's being mouthy, not just the *I'm hungry* sounds that she normally makes when she wakes me. She's never been this aggressive either.

"Jesus, El, what gives?" I groan, sitting up and holding her to my chest so she can't hit me anymore. I stroke her fur for a second before fully taking in my surroundings.

Ryan's not in the room, and my stomach drops. It's not like her to be up before me since the abduction. I jump out of bed and head straight to check the bathroom, finding no sign of her. I walk back through the bedroom and see her phone is gone.

I check my phone and see she sent me a message.

Ryan

I'm downstairs, I'll be up shortly.

With a sigh of relief, I walk back into the bathroom to relieve my bladder and take a quick shower. I step into the hot stream of water and rush through washing off the evidence of last night so I can wrap myself around her again.

A broad smile crosses my face as memories flash through what she wanted last night.

Fuck me, I'm a lucky man.

I'm not sure what came over her or why she decided it was the right time to ask for anal, but god damn. I've done it a few times and yea, it was always great, but jesus, something about Ryan made this a thousand times better.

I turn the water off and hear a loud crash come from downstairs as soon as I step out of the shower. Wrapping a towel around myself, I race out of the bathroom to the stairs. Taking two at a time, I reach the kitchen in record time to see Ryan isn't alone.

<h1 style="text-align:center">Chapter Forty-Eight</h1>

I wake up way too warm. Grey still has me pulled flush to his body, tucked into his muscular form, his arms caging me in. I press a kiss against his forearm before untangling myself from his grasp. Once free, I rush to the bathroom, having to pee so fucking bad my bladder feels like it may actually burst. The instant relief I feel when I finally go is almost as good as the multiple orgasms last night. Almost.

Jesus, I don't know what came over me but I hope it happens again, soon. Having Grey in my ass is something I definitely want to experience again.

I smile happily to no one but myself.

After a quick shower, I throw on one of Grey's t-shirts, grab my phone from the nightstand, and head downstairs to make my man breakfast.

Listen, I'm all about gender equality but if you experienced the orgasms I did last night, you'd be in the kitchen too.

I send a quick message to Grey, letting him know I'm down here so he doesn't worry in case he wakes up before I make it back up with breakfast. I open Spotify and turn on my favorite playlist. The opening chords of *Don't Let Me Down* by The Chainsmokers & Daya start streaming through the phone speakers.

I start swaying and humming along as I pull out the eggs, bacon, and everything else that I could possibly need to make pancakes from scratch. Singing the lyrics out loud along with Daya as I open the cabinet, I bend down to pull out a couple of mixing bowls and place them on the counter before grabbing two pans. I stand back up, placing one pan down and carrying the other with me. I grab a wooden mixing spoon and hold it to my mouth like a microphone, living my best pop star life in this moment when I hear a click and the cold, hard metal of a barrel against my temple. I freeze when a hand is clasped around my mouth from behind in a familiar scene, dropping the pan and spoon.

"You know, the bitch was supposed to kill you, not use you for her own twisted pleasure," a cold voice I've known and detested for years speaks quietly into my ear as she pulls me backward away from the counter.

I have no time to respond when she twists us around to see Grey standing in the doorway, murder in his eyes.

"Nice of you to join us, sexy. I've missed you," Raven purrs in acknowledgment at his arrival.

"I swear to god, you psychotic cunt," he growls. "Let. Her. Go."

"Oh, Greyson, don't speak to me like that. You know you belong to me; she's just been an annoying obstacle since you've been back." She giggles as she presses the gun harder against my temple, the metal digging into my skin.

"Ingrid had been working for me for five years when she first came across this slut a couple years ago." I feel her nod in my direction. "She became obsessed."

Tears prick at my eyes at the torment on his face from seeing me in danger again. I mouth the words, *I love you*, hoping that he understands this isn't his fault.

The look of disgust mixed with horror on his face makes my stomach twist.

"Rave, let her go and I'll leave with you." Grey's voice has turned sickeningly sweet.

"No, the only way you'll leave is if she's out of the picture. Then we can be together the way we were always meant to be," Raven snarls at him in response.

"No, Darlin'. I'll leave with you right now, we can go wherever you want as long as you let go of her." The use of his old pet name for her has my stomach rolling, and

hot tears stream down my cheeks as the exchange continues, unsure if he's saying just what she wants to hear or if he's trying to protect me. My eyes lock on him, searching for answers as they continue speaking to one another as if I'm not even in the room.

"Anywhere?" I can hear the smile in her voice.

Grey nods his head quickly in response.

A sharp pain ignites in my temple and I collapse onto the floor just as the room goes dark. I'm not sure how long I'm out before the kitchen comes back into view. The room is spinning slightly as my eyes flutter open and I see Grey in front of Raven with his hand gripping her throat.

"I want you to hear me, very clearly. The only distraction in this room was you." His voice is venomous, "A distraction I've been trying to forget for the past decade."

I see the gun she was holding on the floor, just within reach. I wrap my hands around the handle, standing up to face the two of them. Grey is still holding onto her throat so tightly she's beginning to turn blue.

"Tarzan," I croak. "Let her go."

He flinches at the sound of my voice, dropping her and rushing over to me. He presses his lips against mine in a chaste kiss, forgetting about Raven's presence for a second. But it's a second too long. She's charging toward us when I step in front of him and raise the gun, squeezing the trigger. A deafening bang echoes around the spacious kitchen just before she falls to the tile floor with a loud thud.

"Something you should have been paying more attention to after the attack. Benny taught me how to shoot." I glare at her limp form. "Bitch."

"Fuck, Ry." Grey takes the gun from me, placing it on the counter behind us, before wrapping me in a tight embrace. "I'm so sorry, baby. I'm so, so sorry." His hand grips my neck, tilting my face just enough for his lips to find mine.

The passion, lust and love in this kiss has my knees buckling under me, completely forgetting the intruder bleeding out on the floor at our feet. I wrap my arms around his neck, pulling him to me, and deepening the kiss. His hands drop, cupping my ass and lifting me to the counter.

"Ry," he groans into my mouth before pulling away. "I need you."

Instead of responding with words, I press my mouth against his again and drop my hands to the towel still tied low around his hips, unwrapping it frantically like a kid on Christmas morning. I cage my legs around him, digging my feet into his ass, urging him forward. His stiff cock slides home as he takes me on the counter in front of Raven's lifeless body. He fucks me hard and fast, with an intensity and need neither of us have experienced before.

"Baby, I need you to come," he groans, reaching between us and pinching my clit.

I scream as a wave of overwhelming bliss crashes over me. As I milk his cock with my release, I feel him swell inside me before he fills me with his seed.

Panting from exhaustion but feeling completely sated, I collapse against his chest as he pulls out and cleans himself with the towel that was around his waist. My face must give away my panic because when Grey's eyes meet mine again, his face falls.

"Ry…" Grey's concern in his voice only does more to sober the orgasmic high I was just in. "What? What's wrong?"

I look up at him and then down at Raven on the off chance that she's still alive.

"We didn't use a condom." My voice cracks as I say the words aloud.

"I— we—" He can't seem to find the words.

"I'm so sorry, I didn't think. I just needed you and I didn't think. I have one more test before I'm in the clear. But what if —" I'm sobbing into my hands. I'm not sure if I'm more terrified of infecting him or getting pregnant and him leaving like my dad did.

"No, Kitten, it's ok. So far, the tests have been negative. Don't go down a rabbit hole." He envelops me in a tight embrace, trying to calm me. "You only have a few more weeks before the final test that they want you to take. It's ok."

"But what if —" I try to catch my breath. "We haven't discussed kids. With the antibiotics, my birth control won't work."

Grey stares at me for a long moment, processing my concern before he speaks. "Kitten, I want what you want. If you want a house full of kids, I'm in. If you want to be child-free. Awesome. If you want to have a house full of Ellie's, I'm ok with that too. The only place I'm drawing a line is a Chihuahua."

I smile at him, unable to say anything else about my concerns about the what ifs, instead grabbing my phone to call Benny who arrives quickly after I explain what happened. The process of being questioned again has me ready to jump out of a window. I get it; being kidnapped and having two people dying suddenly in front of you was a bit suspect. But I've been through enough. I just want to shower and get the hell out of this house, get the hell away from these memories.

Chapter Forty-Nine

One month later

We finally unpacked the last box in our move. Between moving Ryan's photography studio next door to Inkognito, my stuff from Miami, and the few things she wanted to keep from her apartment, it felt like we were drowning in cardboard. After what happened at Jack's, with Ry shooting Raven, it was more than she could bear. I knew I had to get her out of there as fast as possible. Luckily, Joel found us the perfect place. Ellie has made her appreciation quite clear by calling dibs on the large window in the back room overlooking a wooded area.

I come back in from taking the last cardboard box out to the garage and find Ryan sitting on the couch, an e-reader in her hands. She's got a goofy grin on her face which means she's reading a romance and the book boyfriend did something cheesy. I snort as I walk over to her and kneel in front of the couch.

Let's see if I can out cheese him.

"Kitten," I pull her attention from the e-reader when my hand grips her thigh.

"Yea?" She grins at me with a sultry smile.

I smirk, loving that she's always ready for me. "I've been thinking about something." I pause taking in her beauty.

She arches a brow at me in question.

"I've been in love with you since I was twenty years old. It may have taken a decade for us to get here, but the moment I saw you again, standing in Mud House, the walls I had around my heart crumbled." I take her hands in mine, pressing a soft kiss on the back of each one. "There wasn't a day that passed while I was gone that I didn't think about you. Especially when someone brought out a damn Hershey's bar."

I smirk at her and she giggles, her eyes filling with tears.

"I don't want to go another day without you being mine." I dig into my pocket, pulling out the velvet box I've had since I went back to pack up my condo in Miami. I open it and hold it out to her, the black gold band with a pear shaped turquoise diamond set in the middle of a floral design. "Marry me, Ry."

The sharp intake of breath is all I hear before she launches herself at me, her lips crashing hard against mine as we fall back onto the floor. I chuckle into her mouth, gripping her neck, deepening the kiss briefly before pulling back.

"I need an answer, gorgeous."

"Yes, Tarzan. Absofuckinglutely yes!" She giggles, the tears streaking her cheeks. A smile that consumes me breaks across her face just before her lips find mine again.

Later that evening, we're surrounded by our family and friends, celebrating our engagement. I had mentioned to Hadley that I was doing this tonight and she insisted that everyone come over for pizza and beer and I couldn't resist her offer. As close as the girls are, I needed to share this with the friends I have here, the new and lifelong. I'm sitting in the living room with the guys–Connor, Liam, Jack, and Bennett–while the women are all in the back room, I assume looking at things for the wedding. They're all smiles when they re-appear. Ryan's eyes are red like she's been crying again. I raise a brow, but she shakes her head, letting me know she's ok. I pull her onto my lap when she crosses the distance to the couch, holding her close.

By the time everyone leaves, it's late. I can tell she's drained, but something has been on her mind since she came out of the back room earlier.

"Kitten?" I coax her from her thoughts. "Talk to me."

"I –" her voice cuts off for a moment. "What do you think about a courthouse wedding?"

"Baby, I would marry you in the middle of a fucking McDonald's if that's what you wanted." I smile at her.

"Ok," she laughs, shaking her head at me.

Ok, maybe not a McDonald's, but a Chipotle, for sure.

"Good, because I'd like to get married before the baby gets here." She watches me closely as she says the words.

I blink a few times, processing what she's said.

"What?" The smile that takes over my face is so big it hurts my cheeks. "You're? We're?"

She nods shakily as she hands me a pregnancy test with a very bold "PREGNANT" on the digital display.

I engulf her in a hug, spinning us around. I bury my face in her neck, savoring this moment. When I pull back and set her feet back onto the ground, I realize I have tears falling down my face. Ryan has a wide smirk on her face.

"What aren't you telling me?" I ask.

"I may have taken that test a week ago and had bloodwork done to confirm." She giggles as she wraps her arms around my neck, pressing a soft kiss to my lips.

"Ok? And what did the bloodwork confirm?" I ask, my concern now apparent.

"That I'm six weeks pregnant." Her smile is intoxicating. She stays quiet, letting my mind work.

I do the math quickly in my mind and realize what she's trying to tell me.

"It was one of the first times after?" I raise a brow in question, chuckling, already knowing the answer.

She only nods, confirming it. With as safe as we had been up until Raven attacked her, the irony is not lost on me.

We alternate between making love, discussing wedding plans, and deciding which room to turn into the nursery until the sun comes up the next morning. We fall asleep as the morning rays start to break through the curtains, tangled around each other as if we won't survive if more than an inch of us isn't touching.

Epilogue One

T wo weeks later

Not at a McDonald's

Standing in Hadley and Connor's bedroom as a makeshift bridal suite, I touch the small lily necklace that belonged to Grey's mom. He gave it to me this morning before I started getting ready, the gesture making me tear up. It was her favorite necklace. I wish both of our mothers were here with us today. I'm standing in front of a full-length mirror, admiring my floor-length, ocean-blue A-line gown. The deep v-neck with floral laced beading accentuates my growing chest nicely.

The constant need to pee may be annoying, but my tits are living their best life right now.

After several hours of painting on my face–contour, highlighter, a silver smokey eye that would make RuPaul proud– I'm finally ready to get the show on the road.

"You are the most beautiful bride." Hadley fans her face as she starts tearing up again.

She's been an emotional mess since I told her about both the engagement and the baby. She's excited, but I know she wishes that Connor would ask her. He's not getting any younger, and she so desperately wants a family of her own.

"Actually, I think Grace Kelly holds that title." I giggle and bring her in for a hug, flinching slightly, still not used to my breasts being so sensitive.

"OK, you two. Break it up. I need some lovin', too." Pickle snorts as she squeezes in between us, wrapping us both in a hug. "Seriously though, you're gorgeous, babe, and I'm not just saying that because I've seen you naked," she deadpans.

I look between Pickle and Hadley, taking a moment to process what she just said and lose it. I bend at the waist, holding onto the foot of the bed, laughing so hard I can't catch my breath. Hadley starts giggling beside me at the comment and my reaction while Pickle stands there with her hands on her hips.

"I didn't think it was that funny." She pouts.

I stand up after several moments, tears rolling down my cheeks, and stare at her.

"It's not that it was funny. It was random as hell." I step toward her, gently taking her hands in mine. "Why do you keep bringing up seeing me naked or sleeping with women?"

She looks like she's about to tear up.

"Let's go get you married. ok?" She sniffs as she pulls her hands from mine, turning towards the door.

Hadley and I exchange a glance, both of us worried about our friend. Neither of us care that she's into a woman, but the fact that she's hiding something so upsetting she's running away is a big concern. Hadley and I follow Pickle into the hall, where Jack is waiting for us.

His eyes well with tears when he sees me.

"Sis," he breathes, wrapping his arms around me, holding me tight to him.

"We'll be at the door when you're ready." Hadley whispers to me as she and Pickle disappear, leaving Jack and I alone.

"You look just like Mom," he sighs as he releases me. "She would be so proud of the woman you've become. Hell, even the man that asshole has become."

We both chuckle at the second part.

"I miss her so fucking much, Jack. She's missed so much of our lives," I respond softly as I press my hand to my stomach.

I'm not showing yet, but I can't help but hold my baby, thinking about all the things they'll miss out on since all their grandparents are gone.

"I know, sis, but we're in this together, as long as you don't have to live with me again. Knowing you're sleeping with my best friend and hearing it are two very different things." He laughs at me.

I smack his chest. "I hate you."

"You love me." He grins as he hands me a small black box.

I arch a brow as I open it, unsure what to expect. I gasp when I see my mom's silver daisy bracelet, the charm hanging off the dainty chain. We remain quiet as he places it around my wrist. I choke back a sob feeling her presence when it's clasped in place.

"Now, let's get you hitched." He wraps my hand around the crook of his arm and leads me to the back door where Hadley and Pickle are waiting. They nod when they see us and head out onto the patio where everyone is seated. Coming outside, I see Hadley, Connor, and Alannah, with her son, Sean, standing together. The patio is full of lily and daisy flower arrangements. Fresh floral garland is hung strategically along with fairy lights. As I walk further outside, the rest of my family comes into view. Pickle and Clay holding one another. Kayleigh, Liam, Joel, and his husband, Lance, along with their kids.

I barely register that Loki, C, Niall and Dixie are here when we finally round the corner and I see the end of the patio where the rest of my life awaits. My heart swells and

everything else ceases to exist as Jack and I close the distance. My eyes lock on his, those green-gold orbs taking in each inch of my body as I walk closer. I can feel the emotion rolling off of him in waves. When we finally reach him, Jack releases me to Grey, the biggest grin on his face as he takes my hand.

It takes me a moment to realize Benny is standing next to us. I do a double-take when I see he's holding a black book in his hands. I arch a brow and he chuckles at me.

"I did this for you, so just go with it." Benny still has a wide grin on his face.

After our vows, we took a few photos of me and my new husband with our families before I drag Hadley and Pickle into the back room to help me change into a pair of yoga pants and one of Grey's t-shirts.

When I come back out, I find the group gathered around the kitchen table filling plates with burritos, chips and all of the fixin's, including guac and queso. Grey walks up behind me, his arms enveloping me in a warm embrace.

"What is this?" I ask.

He insisted on taking care of the food but I wasn't expecting...

"What? You said no to McDonald's, not Chipotle." His gravelly chuckle sends heat to my core.

I can't help but chuckle.

"I love you, Tarzan." I giggle as I lead him to the fire pit where everyone is seated. I sit next to Kat, wrapping my arm around her. Grey sits on my other side, taking in our surroundings.

Bonus Epilogue

T wo months ago

To: SaraHurstWrites@gmail.com

From: Connor@DLTech.com

Dear Sara

I want to start by sharing, as a forty-two year old Irishman, I'm aware that I am not your typical demographic. With that being said, I am writing to you in hopes you can help me surprise Mo Ghrá. Quite honestly, I probably fell in love with Hadley the moment I first saw her. There is nothing about this woman that isn't perfect in every single way. She has been a fan of your novels since your first book was published. In fact, she has multiple copies in each format.

Though, that may be my doing to make sure she's never too far from a Holt family fix.

She has survived more than any one person should have to experience in a lifetime. Her trauma has helped her grow into a stronger person, and she has even been helping other victims find their way in creating healthy, happy lives. She is thriving despite of all she's been through and I am so incredibly proud of her.

As I said, I've been in love with her since we met. She once told me the day she realized that she had feelings for me was the day I gave her a copy of Finding Each Other to read at my house.

My plan is to propose using the final book in the Love and Survival series.

Would you be able to send a note that I can include in the book?

Thank you for anything you can do,
Connor Quinn.

Dear Connor,

I feel like Mr. Quinn would be too formal between us after all you shared. Your Mo ghrá is a very lucky woman. You might not want just how lucky she is getting out since romance readers can get a bit feral over real-life men who resemble book boyfriends. *wink*

Also, you'd be surprised how many forty-two-year-old men actually read romance novels. There's some good stuff to be found between the pages. You just have to be brave enough to spread them open. *smirk*

As for your request, I think we can do better than a note that you slide into a book, don't you? I believe a set of signed special editions created just for Hadley would be more appropriate.

With Love,

P.S. - I better get an invite to the wedding. You don't want to meet Adam and Brock!

Ryan gives me a nod, the signal for me to make my move.

I clear my throat and stand before our family and friends. "I just want to congratulate the bride and groom." I smile widely at Ryan and Greyson.

"I originally had something different planned but with life, such as it is, I couldn't imagine not sharing this with everyone." I smile, turning to Hadley, pulling her up from where she sits next to me, wrapping her in my arms and pressing a chaste kiss against her lips.

Ryan walks up beside us and hands me the bag she's been hiding for me.

Hadley looks at me, confusion written across her face. I just continue smiling and nod.

"Baby, what?" she asks as she pulls out a book, one she's read many times, however, not the exact copies she's read before.

"Open it, Mo Ghrá," I feel tears already brimming in my eyes as she opens the first book and sees a new dedication.

Finding Each Other

Dedication

To Hadley.

You are one very lucky woman.

Not everyone finds their person.

With Love.

Katie, Jackson, & Sara

She gasps as she looks back at me. I drop to one knee and smile so widely my cheeks hurt.

"Mo Ghrá, finding you was the best thing that has ever happened to me. Every day I wake up, able to call you mine, has been even more incredible than the last. There is so much more in this life I want to experience with you by my side, Mo shíorghrá. Níl leigheas ar an ngra ach posadh." I hear my sister sob at my declaration as I pull out a small black box, flipping open the lid, revealing a four carat emerald cut diamond ring. "Marry me, Mo Ghrá."

"It's taken you long enough." She laughs, tears streaming down her gorgeous face. "Yes, a million times yes. Táim i ngrá leat." The smile on her face as she pulls me back up, crashing her lips against mine takes my breath away. She is the most perfect woman in the world.

I know the cheers of our family are the only things that pull us apart at the moment. Ryan and Kat pull Hadley into a tight embrace. Alannah and Sean hug me before going to Hadley to inspect the ring. I chuckle briefly before Ryan catches my eye with a mischievous look on her face. I arch a brow and she clears her throat.

"Since we're all here, and we have an ordained minister present." She chuckles.

I grin at Hadley who is giggling, nodding her head.

Never in my wildest dreams did I expect to meet the love of my life, at this stage in my existence, but Mo Dhia. I live for the unexpected creature before me and I know our life together will be incredible.

Finding Our Way
Dedication

To Hadley,

Even if you're lucky enough to find that one person, it's not always at the right time or place.

With Love,

Katie, Jackson, & Sara

Finding Us Again

Dedication

To Hadley.

Sometimes, even when the universe aligns, outside forces will do everything they can to pull you apart.

With Love.

Katie, Jackson, & Sara

Finding Our Peace
Dedication

To Hadley,

The stars are aligned.

The outside forces have been eradicated.

Connor is your person.

So, turn around, grab happiness with both

hands and never let go.

With Love,

Katie, Jackson, & Sara

The End.

Before I go onto the exciting projects I have up, I have to give a huge shout- and so much love to Sara Hurst, who not only puts up with my obsession with Jackson & Katie's story but also contributed to this special bonus chapter!

You can check out the first of the Love & Survival Series, Finding Each Other here:

Stay tuned for Pickle's book, an MFF why choose.

swoon

Also by L. Clara

Firework - Prequel MM (Joel and Lance's story) Coming 2025

Endgame - Out now

The Unexpected Series

The Unexpected Match - Out Now Hadley & Connor's Story

The Unexpected First

The Unexpected Second Chance - MFF - Coming Fall 2024

The Unexpected Reunion - Coming TBD 2025

Stand Alone - Dark Romance

KILLER IN OUR POCKET - MFF Coming 7/2024

Stalk me on my socials to find out the most up-to-date information on my projects!

Acknowledgements

My family, your support during this journey has been incredible.

To my Stupid Face Moron, ditto.

My alpha team, you are the MVP, and I can't imagine this journey without you.

Sara - My boo. I'll forever be thankful that you slid into my DM's. You are phenomenal, and I love you!

K.D. - My ride or die, I love you, and I'm so freaking proud of you!

To the FBI Agent who tracks my search history, it's been real.

Lastly, but most definitely not least, to every single one of you who has reached this page. There will never be enough words for me to express my love for you adequately. Thank you for reading my books. I can't wait to share additional stories with you!

About the Author

I'm an introvert. Well, until you get to know me. Then I won't shut up. I'm married to my favorite PITA; he's the doctor to my Clara.

(IYKYK). We have a little boy who is growing way too fast and is already way too smart for my own sanity. I've had an unhealthy obsession with Gilmore Girls and Buffy the Vampire Slayer for years. You'll see the references throughout my writing. I've loved reading for as long as I can remember, but physical books with traditional novel paper give me the ick! So, you'll find me reading on my Kindle or listening to audiobooks on the regular.